# Falling for Trouble

Makayla Cawthorn

# Contents

# Chapter 1

"Riley, you're going to be late if you don't drag your ass out of bed." I rolled over, looking at the time. 6:30. Why did she have to do this to me? I slowly rolled out of bed, making my way out of my room and into the bathroom.

"RILEY!" She yelled from the bottom of the stairs.

"I'm up. Jesus Christ," I said back, more to myself than to her. I took a quick shower. I ran a brush through my hair and wrapped up in a towel. I headed back towards my room. I opened my closet doors, debating what to wear. I decided on a basic dark washed jean, a grey sweater, a grey scarf, and a grey beanie with black flats. After I was dressed, I threw all my school books into my bag and headed downstairs.

"Look who finally listened to me." I ignored her as I grabbed a bowl and dumped cereal into it. "I made eggs, you know." I poured milk into the bowl and sat at the table. "Why can't you ever appreciate a damn thing I do for you?" I rolled my eyes, dropping my spoon in my bowl.

"Because you don't do anything for me. First off, you're a bitch, all the time, and then you go out of your way to impress me by trying to be nice. News flash, it doesn't work like that."

Her jaw dropped. I wasn't sure if she was upset or what, but something was showing on her face.

"You ungrateful bitch." Next thing I knew, a pan was flying at my head. I ducked as it smashed into the wall. I grabbed my bag, leaving my dishes behind, and headed for the door.

It was a long drive to school with the music blaring. I was doing everything I could to keep my mind off of what happened, and the fact that I had to go back there tonight. I was positive that she was going to end up killing me before I graduated. One more year, Riley. One more year. That was probably the only reason I enjoyed being smart. I was able to skip a grade, so I was that much closer to being free.

I pulled into the junior parking lot, which was basically empty, and threw my car into park. Unfortunately, it was only the being of the year. I placed my head in my hands, taking deep breaths, trying to calm down. When I finally felt okay again, I turned my car off and grabbed my bag. I headed down the hill towards the cafeteria, where I knew everyone would be.

"Riley, over here," I heard when I walked in the door. Emmy was sitting in the lounge with a group of girls that I really didn't get along with. When she saw the look on my face, she grabbed her stuff and headed over to me. "I'll catch you guys later," she said with a wave. "Not again," she said with a sad look on her face.

"Yeah, again," I said, quietly. Emmy wrapped me up in a hug, nearly squeezing all the air out of my lungs.

"What happened this time?" I pulled out a chair and plopped down, dropping my bag beside me.

"It was honestly stupid. She bitched because I didn't get out of bed; she bitched because I didn't eat her eggs, and then I told her how it really was, and she chucked a pan at me." Emmy's jaw dropped, and she immediately started feeling my head. "She didn't hit me, Emmy. I knew it was coming." She let out a sigh of relief before sitting down.

"We need to get you out of there. I need you to live through graduation with me!" A small smile cracked on my face. "There's that smile I love to see." I let a real smile out, and Emmy's smile grew. The first bell rang, signaling we had to head to class. "I'll catch you later, okay?" I nodded as I headed in the direction of my class.

The chairs were practically empty; there were a few students buried in their book. I plopped down into a chair towards the back. The second bell rang, and no one else had shown up. I pulled my notebook and textbook out, waiting on the teacher. Someone came running through the door. She was young and looked to be in her mid twenties.

"Sorry I'm late everyone. I'm Ms. Miller, and welcome to calculus." She seemed lost as she spread her papers out across her desk. "Alright, since it's the first day-" she was interrupted by someone walking through the door. The teacher looked just as confused as the rest of us. "And who might you be?"

"Bryson Carter," he said, as he shut the door behind him.

"Well, Mr. Carter, take a seat. We're going to be doing introductions." He nodded and his eyes searched the room. They locked on mine, and a smile spread across his face. He made his way to the back of the room, taking the seat next to mine.

"For the love of god," I mumbled to myself. I kept my focus between my notebook and the teacher as we began introductions.

"Allister," Bryson said. He had his signature smirk on his face.

"We both know this semester will be easier if we just leave each other alone." He chuckled as he leaned back in his seat. Bryson was Emmy's brother, but we despised each other. He didn't like me from day one, and I knew his goal was to make my life a living hell. Luckily the conversation died there, and I could focus.

"Alright class, do the worksheet and I gave y'all, and please, have it done for tomorrow. You're dismissed." I gathered my books and placed them in my bag. I waited for Bryson to leave, but he stayed planted in his seat, so I grabbed my bag and got up. Bryson got up right behind me and followed me out into the hallway.

"What do you want, Bryson?" He smiled at me as we walked down the hall. People were glaring at us left and right. I don't blame them. Bryson was popular, and me? Well, I just did what I had to in order to make it through.

"I just miss my little sisters best friend." I laughed, not because it was funny, but because it was a joke. "Since when were we on a first name basis?" I shrugged my shoulders and kept walking.

"Just doing whatever it takes to get away from you." He laughed, and I kept walking. If he really wanted to talk to me, he could wait until I was at his house. I didn't want shit to start spreading at school.

"How was your first round of classes?" Emmy asked as she set her tray down on the table. I shrugged, taking a bite out of my sandwich.

"I have class with your brother." Emmy's jaw dropped, and then she burst into laughter.

"Lord have mercy on our souls." I busted out laughing. "It's hard enough to have you guys under the same roof, let alone in the same room." She was right. We never failed to argue about something. I think he did it just to piss me off.

"No kidding. This is gonna be the semester from hell." She shot me a sympathetic smile and patted my back.

"Just don't kill each other. I don't know what I would do without you guys." I smirked.

"No promises." The bell rang for lunch to be over. Emmy and I headed towards the trash to put our trays away.

"I'll meet you in the parking lot after school? I need a ride." I nodded, and she gave me a quick hug before running off with some of her cheerleading friends.

A sub on the first day? I thought to myself. We hadn't done anything in this class. We were suppose to be working on homework, but I had completed mine during my study hall. I rested my head on the desk, not wanting to go home but not wanting to be here. When the bell, signaling school was over, rang I grabbed my bag and rushed out to the parking lot. Maybe Emmy had something in mind.

She was already standing by my car when I got there.

"What are your plans for now?" I blurted out without thinking. She laughed.

"Well hello to you too. I don't have anything planned. Don't want to go home?" I shook my head.

"I'd rather spend time with your asshole of a brother before ever going home." Emmy laughed again, pulling me into a hug.

"Well, my house it is."

"Mom, we're home," Emmy yelled as we walked inside.

"Hi, girls," Emmys mom said as she pulled Emmy into a hug.

"Hi, Mrs. Carter," I said with a smile. She wrapped me up in a hug.

"Now, Riley, you know better than to call me that." It was true. I had known the Carter's since we first moved up here when I was in fifth grade. Emmy and I hit it off immediately.

"I'm sorry, momma C." She smiled and kissed me on the cheek.

"Dinner will be ready by five." Emmy and I nodded then ran up the stairs to her room. We dropped our bags and collapsed on her bed.

"There's a party Friday night. You should go," Emmy said, catching me off guard. I didn't go to parties very often, only because I usually wasn't allowed.

"Yeah, I'll try!" Emmy shot me a sympathetic smile.

"I will do anything it takes to keep you out of that house."

# Chapter 2

"**D**id you decide what you were going to wear tonight?" Emmy asked as she got into the car. Bryson usually gave Emmy a ride to school, but I guess lately his head had been shoved so far up his girlfriends ass that he didn't care if she made it to school or not.

"Yeah, I have an idea," I said as I pulled out of her driveway. She smiled at me as I focused on the road. "So Bryson ditched you, again?" I asked, not taking my eyes off the road.

"Yeah. I don't know what he sees in Tamara, but I'm so over it. She's just using him anyway." I shook my head in disgust as I pulled into the school parkinglot.

"He's probably using her too." Emmy laughed and nodded in agreement. It was true. He was captain of the football team, and she was captain of the cheerleading team. They would do anything to keep their image.

"One of them will get hurt, and I'm just going to laugh in his face. They hardly use to hang out. They would just put on a show while they were at school. I don't know what change, but I don't like it." I chuckled and shut off the car.

"Is it bad that it's only the first week of school, and I already don't want to go to calculus?" Emmy laughed as we grabbed our stuff and headed towards the school.

"Is he really that bad?" I nodded and walked.

"I swear he's out to make my life a living hell." Emmy stopped in her tracks with a smirk on her face. I stopped and turned to her, confused as to what was happening. "What?" I asked, clueless.

"You know what they say about boys who are mean to girls?" I shook my head at how childish she was being.

"Don't even go there," I chuckled and started walking again.

"I'm just saying. It all makes sense."

"You're being ridiculous. I'll catch you at lunch." I headed off towards calculus and Emmy waved goodbye. I gave a quick wave back and went into the classroom, taking the seat I had claimed as mine.

"Alright class, let's work on some problems from the work sheet," Ms. Miller said as she sat down at her desk. "Do problems one through ten, and then I will split you into groups to go over it." I pulled the packet out of my notebook and opened my book to the page that explained it. I started writing out the problem the way the book showed me. A paper football came flying at me. It bounced off my face and landed on my papers in front of me.

"What the hell?" I mumbled to myself. I looked around the room. Bryson had a smirk on his face, and I shook my head. I slowly opened the paper football.

You going to the party tonight?

I looked back at Bryson who now had a genuine smile on his face. You didn't see that very often. I nodded at him, going back to my worksheet. I couldn't help but glance over at Bryson here and there. He was perfect in every way possible. Amazing hair, beautiful blue eyes, a perfect smile, flawless skin, and an amazing body. It was rare, but he could be a total sweetheart. That still didn't outweigh how much of an asshole he was 90% of the time. I shook my head, trying to clear those thoughts away.

"Alright class, I'm hoping most of you have completed the ten problems. I will now pair you up so you can compare your answers." I zoned out as Ms. Miller assigned groups until she said my name. "Riley and Bryson, please compare answers." Oh great. I could never get away from him. I looked over at Bryson who, once again, had a smirk on his face. He scooted his chair close to my desk.

"Well hello there, partner."

"I'm never going to make it through the semester." I covered my mouth when I realized I said that out loud. Bryson was doubled over in laughter, practically falling out of his chair. At least I knew I was funny. I shoved my paper in his direction.

"All our answers are different," Bryson said with a frown.

"Pay attention in class and maybe you'd get them right." I wanted the bell to ring to get me out of here.

"Ms. Miller," Bryson said raising his hand. She looked over in our direction with a questioning look on her face. "Riley's not playing nice." I could feel my face flush red as I realized all eyes were on me.

"Riley, you two are suppose to be partners. Be nice, or we will be having a conversation after class." I sighed and placed my head on the desk. Bryson was chuckling to himself.

"You're an asshole," I mumbled as I raised my head back up.

"Old news, dude." Ms. Miller walked over to see how far we had come with comparing answers.

"Well done, Riley. You got them all correct. Mr. Carter, you might want to freshen up on your basic math skills." Now it was my turn to double over in laughter. A senior who got problems wrong because his basic math skills sucked. Bryson shot me a death glare, but I couldn't control the laughter.

"Watch yourself, Allister. I know where you live." I shook my head at him.

"Because I practically live at your house." Finally the bell rang, and I grabbed my stuff, shoving it into my bag. Bryson had already left the room. I headed off to my next class.

"Come on, ladies! Step up your game!" Tamara yelled at the groups of cheerleaders who looked like they were going to pass out. I sat up in the bleachers, working on homework while I waited for Emmy. On the other side of the field, I could see the football players practicing. Bryson was easy to spot, only because they had given him the number one when Scott graduated. Scott was the best player on the team. He had led them to the championship game all four years, banking four trophies. Bryson really hadn't been given the time of day until Scott left. Bryson had been second best, and that wasn't enough for him. Once Scott left, Bryson proved that he was now number one.

"Tamara, don't you think we've done enough for today?" I pulled my attention back to the cheerleaders. Half the team was on the ground.

"Homecoming game is next week. We need to have these cheers perfected! Again!" The team groaned as they got back up and into their starting position. I put my headphones in and focused on my homework.

"Who do you think you are?" A voice asked. I looked up to see Tamara standing over me with her hands on her hips. "You think you're cool because you made Bryson feel like an idiot?" I shook my head at her, not knowing what she was talking about.

"Honestly, Tamara, I have no idea what you're talking about." She laughed.

"I heard what you did to him in math."

"Actually, it was the teacher who said it. I just laughed." She grabbed me by the collar of the shirt and pulled me close.

"Listen here, you don't talk to him, got it? Actually, you don't even look at him. If I find out you did, there will be hell to pay."

"Enough," a voice said from behind Tamara. Emmy came into view, and I couldn't be more happy that she showed up when she did.

"What are you going to do?" Tamara asked. I looked between the two of them. I was thankful for Emmy sticking up for me, but I didn't want to ruin cheerleading because of me.

"Let her go now. I'm sure Bryson would just love to hear about how you upset his baby sister." Tamara mumble something that I couldn't make out and then let go of my shirt, pushing me back against the bleachers.

"This isn't over, Allister." Tamara stormed off the field. Emmy shot me a confused look and I shrugged my shoulders.

"She thinks I made Bryson feel like an idiot in math today." Emmy busted out laughing.

"I heard about that. It was definitely the teacher!" I smiled as I finished packing up my bag. "Now let's go get ready for this party!"

"Are you ready yet?" Emmy yelled at me. I looked in the mirror again, just to make sure I looked okay. I had on a black bandeau with a floral skirt that came up just underneath the bandeau. I pulled on a maroon cardigan and brown boots. I touched up my makeup a bit and re-straightened my hair. When I finally felt I looked okay, I walked out of the bathroom.

"What do you think?" I asked Emmy. Her jaw dropped and she was speechless for a few seconds.

"You look amazing!" I smiled at her kindness. The one thing I never could figure out about Emmy was if she was being honest or not. I felt like, because I was a no one at school, she told me what I wanted to hear to make me feel good about myself. "What's the matter?" Emmy asked, concern showing on her face. My facial expression must have change drastically.

"Nothing, I'm just worried about Tamara," I lied. It was the partial truth. I was worried what Tamara would do if she saw me.

"I got you covered, love. Don't worry about her. If it comes down to it, Bryson is always on my side." I nodded and shot her a smile. She wrapped her arm around mine and we headed out to the car.

The party was in full blast when we got there. The music was bumping, kids stumbling across the lawn, lights flashing in the livingroom. I smiled at the sight.

"Fashionably late. Just how I like it," Emmy said with a smile. I smiled back and we walked into the house. Kids were grinding all over each other, drinks in hand. "Want a drink?" Emmy asked. I nodded and stood around, waiting for her to come back. Emmy came back and handed me a cup filled with what look like beer. I took a sip and smiled as she dragged me to the dance floor.

We danced for what felt like hours before people from the cheerleading team saw Emmy. They ran up, all giving her a hug. I got weird looks from all the girls, but I didn't care. I was having the time of my life with my best friend.

"Emmy, there's a game of truth or dare going on in the game room. You down to play? You can even bring little miss nobody." I rolled my eyes, and Emmy threw her arm around my shoulder.

"Yeah, let's do it!" Emmy grabbed my arm and dragged me off towards the game room. This was going to be fun.

# Chapter 3

Emmy dragged me into the room. I noticed Tamara the minute we walked in. She was sitting next to Bryson with her head on his shoulder. I rolled my eyes at how fake they were. Everyone knew they didn't like each other. Emmy pointed to empty spots on the other side of the circle, across from Tamara and Bryson.

"Well, this just got good," Tamara said with a smirk. Bryson rolled his eyes, not saying a word. There was a bottle in the middle of the circle. It was basically spin the bottle, but instead of kissing the person the bottle landed on, the person who spun it gets to give you a truth or dare. "Who should spin the bottle first?" Tamara asked, looking around the circle. Everyone shrugged their shoulders. "How about Michelle?" Michelle nodded and spun the bottle. It landed on a guy that I didn't know.

"Truth or dare?" Michelle asked the guy." The guy smirked, acting as if he's been dared everything possible.

"Dare." Michelle thought about it for a little while before smiling.

"I dare you to give Tamara a lap dance." The whole group busted out in laughter. Tamara rolled her eyes and sat in a chair. The guy stood up, giving Tamara a lap dance. Her face turned beat red as he shook his ass in her face and grinded on her legs. "Times up," Michelle called. The group still laughing.

"I'm so glad I got that on camera," some kid said. Once again the group busted out in laughter. Tamara looked extremely embarrassed. It was now Tamara's turn to spin the bottle. She gave it a good spin, and it spun for a while. When it finally began to slow down, people were guessing who it was going to land on. The bottle stopped, pointing directly at me. A smile formed on Tamara's face.

"Truth or dare?" She asked, still smiling. I thought about it for a little while and the group started chanting.

"Dare, dare, dare!" No one thought I would have balls enough to do it.

"Dare," I said as the group went into an uproar. They weren't being mean though. In a way, it seemed like they were encouraging me to break out of my shell. Tamara seemed surprised that I actually went through with it.

"Okay then," she said, sitting in silence for a minute. "I dare you to kiss Bryson, on the lips." Bryson's head shot up from his phone, and we exchanged glances. I looked at Emmy, who gave me a nod. I walked over to Bryson, who looked just as surprised as I felt. I couldn't believe I was going to do this. I was about to kiss the person I disliked the most. I took a deep breath before placing my lips on his. He wrapped his fingers in my hair, kissing me back. I knew it was all a show to piss Tamara off. We were both breathing heavy when he finally pulled away.

"Ow ow," one of Bryson's friends said. The group was cheering, and Bryson and I busted out into laughter.

"What the fuck was that?" Tamara asked Bryson as I took my seat again.

"She kisses better than you," was all Bryson had a chance to say before the group started yelling in excitement. I looked over at Emmy who looked surprised, but was laughing. She nudged me in the arm and gave me a smile.

The game went on for a while before people started to break away to get more drinks and dance. I took a sip out of my cup, realizing it was empty.

"I'm gonna go get another drink. Do you want one?" Emmy nodded. "I'll meet you out on the dance floor," I said before walking out to the kitchen.

"Chug, chug, chug," I heard as I walked into the kitchen. Some kid was being held upside down on top of the keg. He raised his hand, signaling he was done drinking. When they set him down, he stumbled all over the place before releasing his stomach contents on the floor. The guys who were holding him up started laughing. I filled mine and Emmy's cup and headed out to the dance floor. She waved me down when she spotted me. I handed her the drink and started dancing along to the music.

I knew the alcohol was starting to catch up with me. The room was beginning to spin, but I kept dancing. I felt someone's hands on my waist, and I didn't care. I grinded on whoever was behind me. Pretty soon, I felt something poking me, and I was sure it wasn't his hands. I turned around to see Bryson. I had been dancing with Bryson this whole time, and

I turned him on? I was imagining things, or the alcohol was really getting both of us. I could feel the alcohol threatening to come back up.

"Excuse me," I said as I ran off the dance floor and into the bathroom. I closed the door and dropped to the floor in front of the toilet. Instantly, I started releasing all the alcohol from my stomach. I heard the bathroom door open, and someone was holding my hair. After five minutes of violently getting rid of the alcohol, my body released itself. I fell back, my butt hitting the floor. I took deep breaths trying to calm myself. I felt someone rubbing my back.

"Let's get you home," the all too familiar voice said. I couldn't place who it was, and I didn't care. I just wanted to get home.

The next morning, I woke up with a pounding headache. I laid in bed, keeping my eyes closed. The sunlight was only making it worse. I could hear my phone vibrating on the night stand, but I wasn't in the mood to check it. Before I knew it, I drifted back to sleep.

"Riley Allister, if I have to come in here one more time to wake you up, you're going to regret it." I pulled the pillow over my head. The sound of her yelling was making my head pound.

"Get out," I mumbled through the pillow. The pillow was ripped off my face and a hand connected to my cheek. "What the fuck?" I yelled.

"Who do you think you are talking to me like that?" I got out of bed and went into the bathroom, slamming the door closed. I was not in the mood to deal with this right now. I ran some water over my face then looked in the mirror. My cheek was turning red. She started banging on the door.

"Go away," I yelled. Finally, the banging stopped. I waited a few more minutes before opening the door. She was no where in sight. I headed back to my room. I remembered my phone had been going off nonstop earlier, so I decided to check it. I had a bunch of texts and missed calls from Emmy.

Emmy- where are you?

Emmy- Riley, where did you go? I saw you run off the dance floor.

There were more like it, but the last one caught my eye.

Emmy- please let me know that you're still alive and that someone didn't kidnap you and murder you.

I chuckled a little, but I felt bad that I made Emmy worry that much. Last night, I didn't think to let her know I was leaving. Hell, I don't even remember how I got home, and apparently it wasn't from Emmy.

Riley- I'm so sorry. Last thing I remember is dancing with someone and running to the bathroom. I don't even remember coming home.

I set my phone back down on the night stand and decided to get ready.

"You have no idea how happy I was to hear from you," I chuckled and took a sip of my coffee. My headache was finally starting to go away. Emmy sat across the table from me, shooting me a dirty glare.

"I'm sorry I worried you. You saw me; I really wasn't in the right state of mind." She laughed, nodding in agreement. Emmy paid for our coffees and we headed out of Starbucks.

"Oh boy," Emmy said. I looked at her, confused as to what she was talking about. When I looked ahead, I saw Tamara walking towards us.

"Oh boy is right." Tamara got right up in my face, staring me down.

"You're going to pay for what happened last night." I laughed at her stupidity.

"It was your stupid dare." She shot me a death glare.

"I'm not talking about that. I'm talking about you dancing with MY boyfriend, and then leaving the party with him." I looked at Emmy, just as confused as she was. "You're going to pay," she said, then walked away.

# Chapter 4

Emmy and I busted out into laughter as Tamara walked away. I still had no idea what had happened at the party.

"What the hell did I do last night?" Emmy shrugged her shoulders with a smile on her face. I knew she knew more than she was saying. "You better spill it," I said.

"Spill what? I know nothing." I laughed. She would end up telling me. "So how's the wicked witch?" I shrugged my shoulders. I didn't want to tell Emmy about how she slapped me, but I knew she would get it out of me.

"It was a complete shit show this morning." Emmy touched my cheek, and I winced at the pain.

"What did she do?" I looked down.

"I didn't want to get up and she slapped me." Emmy looked at me, concern flooding her face.

"I'm not kidding; I'm going to get you out of there. Stay at my house tonight." I nodded in agreement.

The house was dark when I got home. It was unusual, but it probably meant she wasn't home, and I was okay with that. I headed up to my room and started packing things.

"Where do you think you're going?" I jumped at the sound of her voice, but I ignored her, continuing to pack. She threw my bag across the floor.

"What do you want?" I asked. I could feel the anger building up inside of me.

"I asked you a question." I picked my bag up off the floor, throwing the rest of my clothes into it.

"I don't need to tell you anything." I zipped up my bag and threw it over my shoulder, grabbing my school bag as well.

"I am your guardian, and you will respect me." I laughed and she looked at me, confusion taking over her face.

"That's all you are. If it wasn't for you being married to my dad, and my dad stating that you would be my guardian if he died, then you wouldn't be. You're nothing but a worthless drug addict that uses the money my dad left, for me, for drugs. In my book, you are no where close to being a guardian." I walked down the stairs.

"I'm not done with you!" She yelled to me, running down the stairs.

"Well, I'm done with you." I went to open the door, and I heard something smash against the wall. I walked out the door, slamming it behind me.

Emmy was waiting outside when I pulled in. Tears were running down my face. She ran over to me, pulling me into a hug.

"What happened?" I sobbed into her shoulders as she kept hugging me.

"That bitch is going to end up killing me some day." Emmy rubbed my back and gave me a supportive smile. I knew she was going to be here to help me through everything.

"My mom has the guest room set up for you." I smiled as she led me inside. Momma C wrapped my up in a gig the minute she saw me.

"You stay here as long as you need, got it?" I nodded as Emmy dragged me to the guest room. "Dinner will be done in a half hour, girls!" She yelled up to us.

The guest bedroom was huge but plain. The walls were painted a darker blue and had white curtains. There was a twin size bed with a lighter shade of blue for the comforter. The walls were bare other than the dresser with a flat screen on it and a mirror.

"Well, what do you think?" I shrugged my shoulders, not really sure what to say. I was so grateful the Carter's were letting me stay here.

"I like it. It's just different from home, you know?" Emmy nodded in agreement. I had stayed in this room multiple times, but it was basically mine now.

"Once you decide what you want to do, this room is all yours, and you're free to decorate it as you please," Emmy said with a smile. She gave me a quick hug. "We better get ready for dinner."

"...I swear, one of my clients was on something. It was too weird!" Momma C had been telling us about her day at work as we ate dinner. She was a lawyer, and she dealt with some serious weirdos.

"Sounds like an interesting day, honey," Mr. C said with a laugh. As nice as it was to be in an actually family again, it broke my heart knowing it wasn't my family.

"Has anyone seen Bryson? I haven't been able to get ahold of him," momma C asked. Emmy and I shook our heads. Momma C knew that Bryson and I didn't get along, so I would be the last person to know where he was.

"I'm here, mom. Sorry," Bryson said as he walked through the door. He set his stuff down and took his place at the table. His eyes scanned the room, and a smirk came on his face when he locked eyes with me. I could feel the heat from the blush making its way to my face. I looked down at my plate to get away from the tension.

"Bryson, Riley will be staying with us for a while," momma C told him. He nodded, not saying a word. Was that bad thing? We hadn't talked about what happened at the party, and honestly, that was fine by me.

"So the girls from the cheerleading team want me to go to some party with them. You're more than welcome to come," Emmy said as she stood in my door way.

"No, thanks though. I think I'm gonna work on unpacking." Emmy nodded in agreement and left. I opened up my suitcase, sorting my clothes to put away.

"Finally got sick of your stepmother?" I jumped at the sound of his voice. I turned around to see Bryson standing in my room.

"You know?" He nodded his head.

"It's not hard to know when you're friends with my sister. She worries about you." I turned around to finish unpacking.

"I know she worries," I said, trying not to cry. Bryson was right by my side, wrapping me in a hug. I hugged him back, letting the tears roll down my cheeks. "I'm sorry," I said as I pulled away, realizing I drenched his shirt with tears.

"Don't be. Sometimes you just need to let it out," he said with a chuckle. "I'm right down the hall if you ever get sick of my sister." I nodded my head and he left. What just happened? Bryson was actually nice to me for once.

# Chapter 5

"Riley, time to get up." I woke up to someone shaking me. "You have school today." I opened my eyes and looked to see who was standing above me. It was momma C.

"I must have forgotten to set my alarm." She gave me a smile and walked out. I rolled out of bed and searched through my clothes. I found a pair of dark wash skinny jeans with a blue button front shirt. I tucked my shirt in and put on a brown belt completing my outfit with a pair of light brown boat shoes. I curled my hair and put on light makeup. After getting ready, I headed down stairs.

"Good morning," Emmy sang as I walked into the kitchen. I sat down across from her at the table after grabbing a glass of orange juice.

"Morning," I said, still trying to get the sleep away. Momma C set a plate of pancakes in front of me. I poured some syrup on them and devoured them. It wasn't often that I got a nice breakfast.

"Hurry up, girls. You don't want to be late," momma C said with a smile. Emmy and I finished our breakfast and headed out.

"My car?" I asked as we made it to the driveway. Emmy nodded and we got into my car, heading to school.

"Okay class, get into your pairs again," Ms. Miller said. Bryson dragged his chair over to my desk. I was not in the mood to deal with school today. Bryson looked at my paper and noticed it was blank.

"Did we finally go over something that ms smarty pants doesn't understand?" Bryson asked with a smile. All I wanted to do was bang my head against the desk.

"I'm not in the mood, Bryson." He gave me a confused look, but said nothing more.

"Riley Allister, could you please report to the deans office," someone said over the intercom. People instantly started talking. Probably wondering what I did to get in trouble. I ignored them and packed up my bag. I looked at Bryson who seemed just as confused as me and the rest of the class. I shrugged my shoulders at him and walked out. The halls were bare as I made my way to the admissions office. People were looking at me weird when I walked into the office.

"The dean is waiting for you in his office," the secretary told me. I headed towards his door, which was closed. I knocked a couple times, waiting for an answer.

"Come in," he yelled. I pushed the door opened to reveal two police officers standing before the dean.

"You wanted to see me?" I asked, nervously. He motioned for me to have a seat.

"Riley, I'm officer Allan. We just have a few questions." I looked at him, confusion written all over my face, I'm sure. "Is

Angela Allister your guardian?" It hit me then. She was trying to get back at me for walking out.

"Yes, why?"

"She called in a missing persons report this morning." I shrugged my shoulders.

"I thought the person had to be missing for more than forty eight hours?" I questioned. I had taken a few criminal justice classes online when I had become interested in crime, thanks to law and order.

"Usually yes, but she said there was an argument, and she was afraid you were going to hurt yourself." I was no longer scared; I was pissed.

"Are you kidding me? She doesn't care what I do or where I am." I sat back in the chair, trying not to cry.

"You guys aren't very close?" The officer asked. I shook my head no.

"The only reason she is my guardian is because my dad made it that way before he died. We don't like each other. Hell, we don't even get along." The officer nodded and jotted some notes down. "Honestly, I don't feel safe there, that's why I'm staying at my friends. She's just doing this to try and show that she cares about me, but she doesn't." The officer wrote more down before sighing.

"Unfortunately, you have to go back home. We will look into it, but only if you want us to." I shook my head, kindly declining his offer. "Well, heres my card just in case." He handed me a business card with his name, rank, and number on it.

"Thanks," I said. "Am I free to go?" The officers nodded and I looked at the dean for comfirmation. He nodded his head as well, and I left.

The cafeteria was packed as kids filed in for lunch. I was getting looks from everyone, and I tried to brush them off. I rested my head in my hands, hoping that this day didn't get any worse.

"What's up, buttercup?" Emmy asked as she sat down. I shrugged my shoulders, not really wanting to talk about what happened. "You know I'm here when you're ready to talk." I nodded. She knew me too well.

"Well, well, the trouble maker herself," Bryson said walking over. I could see the look of worry cross Emmys face.

"Not the time, Bryson," I said, not bothering to look up. I heard a tray hit the table, and I looked up to see Bryson sitting down. I looked at him, confused as to what was happening. "What? I'm not allowed to change my seat here and there?" I let out a small laugh, and a smile formed on Bryson's face. Emmy looked between the two of us.

Bryson was able to keep us entertained during lunch period, making me hate him less every time he talked. I started gathering my stuff, knowing the bell was going to ring soon.

"What do we have here?" Tamara asked, standing behind Bryson.

"Well, it's lunch, so we're eating?" Bryson said. Emmy and I busted out laughing, Tamara shooting us a death glare.

"Why are you sitting with these losers?" She asked, rubbing his back. He shrugged her off.

"Watch it. That's my sister you're talking about. Last time I checked, I didn't have to tell you what I was doing." Tamara rolled her eyes. "Now if you'll excuse me, I'm walking these ladies to class." Bryson stood up and motioned for us to follow him. What the hell was going on with him?

# Chapter 6

I stared out the window as Emmy pulled into my driveway. I had left my car at her house incase anything happened, then I would have a reason to leave. I could see her standing in the doorway, waiting for me. I knew she was angry. I don't care what kind of front she was putting on right now, the minute we were behind closed doors, all hell would break loose.

"You call me if you need anything. You know you're more than welcome to come stay with us anytime," Emmy said with a smile. I gave her a quick hug before getting out of the car and grabbing my stuff from the car. Angela ran up to me, giving me a hug.

"I was so worried about you. You scared me half to death," she said. I shrugged her off of me.

"Emmy knows we hate each other. You don't have to put on a show." Angela gave me a death glare and watched as Emmy pulled away.

"You're an ungrateful bitch, you know that?" I couldn't contain the laughter that escaped my lips.

"You turned me into what I am," I said as I pushed past her and headed into the house. I wasn't going to death with her bullshit.

"Riley, I'm not done talking to you! You will respect me. I'm your guardian." I stopped, dead in my tracks. I turned around to face her, staring her in the eyes.

"Don't pull that card on me. You could care less what happens to me. All you want is my fathers money to support your drug habits." Her mouth dropped, and I could tell I had pissed her off.

"Who do you think you are? I'm like this because of losing your father. That was hard on me to, you know." Once again, the laughter escaped from my mouth.

"You were a drug addict long before you met my father. You only married him for his money. You would say you're going out shopping, but really, you went a bought drugs. He wasn't stupid. He knew, but he loved you." I could see the tears starting to roll down her cheeks. I knew I hit a nerve, but she deserved it. Maybe reality would knock her in the face. She turned away from me and walked out of the room. I headed up to my room, hoping that would be the last of her for the night.

For once, I was woken up by the sound of my alarm clock and not Angela. I rolled out of bed, heading to the bathroom. The house was quiet, but I liked it that way. It probably meant that Angela had gone out last night and didn't bother to come home. Once I was done getting ready, I went back to my room, grabbing my phone to call Emmy.

"Good morning, sunshine." I chuckled. I never understood how she was so bubbly in the morning.

"Morning. Do you mind giving me a ride to school?" There was a brief pause on the other end.

"I'm pulling into your driveway now. I figured you'd need a ride since your cars at my house," she said with a laugh. The line clicked dead, and I grabbed my bag, running out the from door. To my surprise, Bryson was sitting in the passenger seat of her car. I got in the back, making sure I was sitting behind Emmy.

"Thank you," I said to Emmy with a smile.

"There is a reason I'm your best friend." We laughed as she drove to school.

"So you have to move like numbers to the same side?" Bryson asked. He seemed truly confused, and I couldn't help but feel bad for him. This was basic algebra, and we were in calculus.

"Yes, so say you have an equation like $2x-5=7+6x$. You would move the x's to the same side and the real numbers to the same side, but don't forget they go from positive to negative, or vice versa when they move sides." Bryson wrote the equation down, struggling through it.

"This shit is too hard." I chuckled at the sight of him struggling. The big, bad football captain couldn't figure out basic algebra.

"How did you make it to senior year?" I said with a laugh. He shot me a glare and I kept laughing. "Listen, if it really means that much, I can come over and help you with your math skills." A smile took over his face.

"You would do that?" I nodded, doing the problem out and showing him.

"Oh, that's the answer." I laughed.

"How was class?" Emmy asked, walking over to the table.

"It was quite funny seeing your brother struggle." She shook her head with a smile on her face.

"You would get enjoyment out of that." I nodded, taking a bite out of my sandwich.

"I offered to help him with his math." Emmys mouth dropped, food almost falling out.

"Have pigs learned to fly yet?" I laughed, shaking my head.

"I kind of felt bad that he didn't understand basic algebra. I mean, we are in calculus, and if he doesn't understand it, he'll never pass his senior year." She smiled, taking a bite of her lunch.

"Aw, Riley does have a heart." I threw a carrot at her and busted out laughing.

"Watch it, or else your brother will replace you as best friend," I said with a laugh.

"I thought I already was," Bryson said, showing us his puppy face. We laughed at him. "So, Riley, come over tonight and help me with math?" Bryson asked, once again giving me the puppy dog face.

"I guess I could do that." A smile formed on his face as he took a bite of his lunch.

"We do have a test tomorrow, and I can't afford to fail. If I fail then there's no playing in the game Friday night." I chuckled.

"I love how the only reason you want to pass is so you can play football."

"What is going on with you and Bryson?" Emmy asked as we walked to we car.

"What do you mean?" I said, clueless as to what she was talking about.

"You guys have actually been nice to each other. Ever since the party." I still hadn't found out what happened at the party, and I hadn't been able to get it out of Emmy.

"I didn't sleep with him, did I?" I asked, causing Emmy to laugh. She shook her head no, still laughing. "Then why won't you tell me what happened?" I whined.

"That would take the fun out of torturing you," she said with a smile. "Don't worry, it was nothing bad. I'm just glad you two are finally getting along." We walked in silence the rest of the way to her car. She was right; it was nice to finally get along with Bryson and not to always be at each other's throats, but what happened that night to cause us to be nice?

# Chapter 7

I sat at the table, watching as Bryson struggled through the problem. He was still trying to get the hang of basic algebra.

"So I move the x's to the same side, and the regular numbers to the same side?" I nodded as he did the work for the basic problem. I had given him the most simple problem I could. "Okay, now that I'm down to one number on each side, what do I do?" I chuckled.

"You divide the number that's attached to the x by the other number number and whatever that comes out to be is what x equals, get it?" He shook his head and did as I said.

"Did I get it right?" I looked over his work, using the calculator to check. I smiled when my math worked out to the same numbers he had.

"That's right!" Bryson jumped up and did a happy dance. I wrote out a couple more problems on a paper and handed it to him.

"Now do these to prove you actually understand it. I'm not going to help you with these. I'll check your answers when you're done." He gave me a sad look when I said I wouldn't help him, and I couldn't help but laugh. This kid never did things on his own; that was for damn sure.

A little while later Bryson shoved the paper over to me, smiling. I looked over his oaoer, doing the quick math for each problem.

"One hundred," I said with a laugh. Once again, Bryson did a happy dance around the dinning room. I shook my head. This kid was ridiculous.

"Thank you, Riley. Obviously I wouldn't pass calculus without knowing this." I smiled at him. "But, can we save the harder problems for another day? My brain hurts." We both busted out laughing.

"Now, that doesn't surprise me, but yes, we can wait for another day." He smiled, giving me an awkward hug as I was sitting. I raised my eyebrow at him when he pulled away.

"What? I can't give me tutor a hug because she helped me understand something?" I shook my head with a smile on my face. "Let's go get food; I'm starving." I nodded in agreement and stood up.

I took a bite out of my pizza as Bryson laughed at something he saw on Facebook.

"You're gonna kill all your brain cells, and you're going to forget everything I just taught you," I said, shaking my head.

"Guess you'll just have to tutor me more often," he said with a laugh. I finished off my pizza, wiping a napkin across my face to make sure I didn't have any sauce on it.

"You put down food like a guy," Bryson said with a raised eyebrow. I chuckled, taking a sip of my drink.

"I haven't eaten anything all day," I argued back.

"It's kind of hot," Bryson said, catching me off guard. I shook my head, taking another sip.

"Now I remember why I don't hang out with you." I laughed as Bryson placed a hand over his heart.

"Ouch, that hit hard." I laughed harder, causing me to snort. I covered my mouth, extremely embarrassed, and Bryson busted out into laughter. It was obvious he couldn't control it. I could feel my face turning beat red. I threw the closet thing I could find, a straw, at Bryson. "That wasn't very nice," he said, rubbing where the straw hit him.

"It was just a straw, you big baby," I said. He glared at me as he grabbed an ice cube out of his drink.

"Are you seriously just going to eat that?" I asked, slightly confused. He shook his head and threw it at me. It landed down my shirt, and I shot him a death glare, not wanting to dig it out in public.

"That's got to be cold. Are you just going to leave it there until it melts?" I nodded, smirking at him. "Well then, let me help you out." Bryson leaned across the table, reaching his hand down my shirt and grabbed the ice cube before I even had a chance to say anything. I looked at hin, shock written all over my face. I then watched as he placed the ice cube in his mouth.

"You're sick," I said, shooting him a disgusted look. He smiled and took a sip of his drink. The waitress brought out bill over, setting it on the table.

"Look who we have here. The two love birds." How had I not noticed Tamara working here? I looked down at the table, trying to ignore her.

"Cut your shit, Tamara. We just want to pay our bill." She laughed.

"Bryson Carter is actually going to pay for a date?" She said, laughing again.

"It's not a date," I said, finally getting the courage to fight back. Bryson shot me a look as I threw money on the table. I stood up and grabbed my stuff, waiting for Bryson. "Keep the change," I told Tamara as we headed out. I saw a guy, who was wearing a nicer shirt than the other employees, and I assumed he was the manager. "Your worker has awful customer service." I pointed back towards Tamara and kept walking. I heard the manager call her over, and I hoped she was getting fired.

"That was bold, Allister. Nobody talks back to Tamara." I shrugged my shoulders, sliding into the passenger seat of his car.

"Someone needed to do it," I said, looking out the window. Bryson laughed.

"To your house?" He asked as we left the parkinglot. I nodded and he headed in the direction of my house.

"You did what?" Emmy asked, obviously surprised. I laughed.

"I told her off, and I managed to buy your brother food." She chuckled on the other end of the phone.

"He's always open to people buying him food, idiot. I just can't believe you told Tamara off! She's gonna make you pay for it." I laid back on my bed, putting Emmy on speaker phone.

"Whatever, she'll be gone next year." I heard Emmy chuckle.

"Yeah, might as well make a name for yourself now," she said, and I laughed. "Hey, there's a party this Friday. Come with me?" Emmy asked. I thought about it for a minute before answering.

"Fine, but you have to tell me what happened with me and Bryson at the last party." She was silent for a little bit.

"I suppose I could do that, but I really have to go. Dinner calls."

"I hate you," I said.

"I love you," she said with a laugh, and the line clicked dead.

# Chapter 8

I sat in a chair while Emmy did my hair and makeup. She put on light makeup to bring out my features and curled my hair. I looked in the mirror, amazed at the work she did.

"Go put your dress on. We don't want to be late," Emmy said, way too excited to get to the party. I went into the bathroom, stripping my sweatpants and t-shirt and put on a dress that was deep red on top with some jewels and had a see through black skirt. It had a short slip underneath. I slid on some basic black high heels and grabbed a small purse that had a shoulder strap. I walked out into my room and Emmys jaw dropped.

"What do you think?" I asked, clearly knowing what she was going to say. She motioned for me to spin around, and I did so.

"Riley," she paused for a minute. "You look amazing!" She said, a smile forming on her face. I didn't think the dress had looked that good on me. It did fall in all the right places though. For being thin, I did have some curves, and this dress definitely showed them.

"You ready to go?" I asked, kind of wanting to get the night over with. She nodded and we headed out.

"It's only nine, and people are already hammered," Emmy said, sounding disgusted. I chuckled.

"Are we any better? We are here to get drunk and it's only nine." We walked in silence for a bit before Emmy answered.

"No, because we're not already sloshed. These people have probably been gone since they arrived." We laughed as we walked into the house. We basically came to the same house to party every time. I'm surprised the cops haven't found it yet. The house was bumping with music and people dancing all over each other, just like every other party. "Drinks?" Emmy asked. I nodded in response and leaned against the wall waiting for her. I admired the people dancing around, drinking, and just having a good time. Although we were all in different groups, we all came together at parties; well, almost everyone.

"God, what are you doing here?" Tamara said with an eye roll. I was really getting sick of her attitude and hate towards me when I hadn't really done anything to her. Well, other than what went down in the pizza house. I smiled at the memory, almost forgetting she was standing in front of me. "Well, are you going to say anything?" She said, pulling me out if my thoughts.

"Who dressed you?" Seriously? That was the best that I could come up with? I mentally slapped myself, but noticed how offended she seemed. Well, that went better than I expected. She was wearing a short, strapless, sparkly silver dress that hit right under her butt. If she bent over, she would be showing the world the nasty thing that guys were somehow still attracted to.

"This so happens to be my mothers dress from her high school years," she defended. I chuckled. I couldn't imagine her mother ever wearing something like that. Her mother was practically head of the church. Full blown Christian, and she worshipped God like no other.

"You might not want to bend over too far," I said, pointing out that no one wanted to see what was under there. A smirk appeared on her face.

"You all would like that, wouldn't you?" Her smirk grew into a creepy smile, and I wanted to walk away. I had enough of her tonight; I just wanted to enjoy my night.

"No one wants to see that," a random voice said. "It's used and abused; almost like throwing a hotdog down a hallway." The crowd busted out into laughter, and Bryson appeared next to her. I couldn't stop laughing, grabbing my stomach, fighting for air. I knew Bryson could be a jerk, but I never expected him to say that to his girlfriend. Tamara gave him a death glare before storming away.

"Dude, Bryson, that was awesome," a drunk kid said as he stumbled over. Emmy came back, handing me my drink. I was finally able to stop laughing, but I was still trying to catch my breath.

"What did I miss?" Emmy asked, looking around at the circle that had formed. I started laughing again, thinking back to what happened. Emmy just stared at me, confusion all over her face. I took a sip of my drink, telling her what her dear brother did. "Are you serious?" Emmy said, busting out into laughter. I nodded my head, knowing I wasn't going to control the laughter.

I hadn't seen Tamara the rest of the night. I wonder if Bryson's little comment caused her to leave the party completely. Not that I was complaining. The party seemed to be doing just fine without her. I was leaning against the wall, sipping on my drink, while Emmy was dancing with the cheerleaders. I didn't want to get so drunk to the point where I didn't remember what happened, again.

"Can I crash your one man party?" I looked around, wondering where that came from, and then I noticed Bryson leaning against the wall next to me.

"Yeah," I said with a small smile. "Thanks for earlier." Bryson chuckled at the memory.

"I walked over at the right time. You had set that up perfectly." I smiled, taking another sip. "Taking it slow tonight?" He said, nodding his head at the cup in my hand.

"Yeah, I would like to remember this party," I said with a laugh. I'm sexy and I know it came bumping over the speakers and Bryson started screaming. I raised my eyebrows at him, watching him dance around. Yup, he was a guy alright. He grabbed my hand and pulled me in to dance with him.

"Let me walk you to Emmys car," Bryson said with a smile. I nodded in agreement and followed him out of the house. We had spent the past few hours dancing to every song that came on. Neither one of us were too drunk, and it was nice. This was nice; actually being able to get along.

"Thanks for tonight," I mumbled. I had never felt nervous around Bryson before, but after everything that had been happening lately, I was always careful to make sure what I said wasn't stupid. Bryson smiled and wrapped his hand around mine, intertwining our fingers. In that moment, I could feel the chills go through my body, and the butterflies were fluttering in my stomach. "I'm sure I would have just stood against the wall the whole night."

"We wouldn't have wanted that, now would we?" I chuckled and shook my head. Emmy was already waiting in her car when we walked up. She waved at me, and I gave her a wave back. Bryson walked to the passenger side, opening the door for me. As I went to sit down, he pulled me back and wrapped me in a hug. The chills went through my body again. This felt right, being wrapped in his arms in that moment. He placed a kiss on my cheek and let me get into the car. He gave us a quick wave before Emmy drove off.

"What was that?" Emmy asked with a grin. I shrugged my shoulders, still not sure as to what happened. What was it about Bryson Carter that was making me feel like this now?

# Chapter 9

Once again, my head was throbbing. I knew I hadn't drank much the night before, nor had I gotten into a fight, so why did my head hurt? I rolled over to look at my phone. Quarter past ten, and texts from Emmy.

Emmy- hey dinner tonight at 6. Momma wants you there ;)

I smiled; I loved knowing that these people actually cared for me. I know for a fact momma C would take me in as her own in a heart beat.

Riley- I'll be there at 3! :)

I wrote Emmy a quick text back and headed off for the bathroom. What was I going to do until three? I hoped in the shower, washing the grime from last nights party off of me. Once I was out of the shower, I went back to my room, searching for an outfit. After about five minutes of not being able to decide, I grabbed the closest thing to me, which just so happened to be a floral sun dress that hit mid-thigh on the front and went past my knees in the back. I started to put the dress on before I got distracted by my phone vibrating on the night stand. I walked over and picked it up, seeing a text from Bryson. Well, that's weird.

Bryson- wanna chill before you come over for dinner?

I could feel my heart beat quickening inside my chest. Bryson wanted to chill? I stared at my phone a while longer before I realized it would be a good idea to reply.

Riley- would love to. I'm ready whenever.

With that, I did my hair and make up quickly, not really caring how I looked. The pounding in my head had completely vanished, and I was ready to take on the day.

"Snack bar sound okay?" Bryson asked as I slid into his passenger seat.

"Sounds great. I'm really feeling some ice cream." Bryson chuckled as he put the car in drive and took off. I watched out the window as the scenery changed from city to country. That was the nice thing about South Carolina; there were big, and small, cities all over the place, but you didn't have to go far to find the peaceful country. As Bryson drove, my interest changed from the landscape to him. I couldn't help but admire how handsome he was. Perfectly tanned skin, flawless, bright blue eyes, gorgeous smile, and an amazing jaw line; he was definitely the boy that mothers warn their young daughters about.

"What kind of ice cream?" Bryson asked, breaking the long silence that filled the car ride. I thought about it for a second while looking at the options.

"Black raspberry," I said with a smile. Bryson walked up, ordering for both of us. He wrapped his arm around my shoulders as we waited for our ice cream. Every couple of seconds I would look at him, trying to understand everything that happened the last couple of weeks. Once our ice cream came out, Bryson grabbed it, handing me mine.

"Let's go for a walk?" Bryson asked. I nodded in agreement and we headed towards the park just down the road. Once again, it was silent, but it wasn't an awkward silence. I licked my ice cream was we walked. "Looks like you could do wonders with that tongue," Bryson said, causing me to choke on my ice cream and him bursting into laughter.

"So not funny," I said, pushing him. He was like a wall; he didn't move at all. Once he stopped laughing, he grabbed my hand in his. What is going on? Although I liked the idea of us being nice to each other, I still wasn't use to it. We had gone years being down right mean to each other. Once we got to the park, we sat down on a bench, finishing our ice cream. I wanted to ask him about the party, and everything that had gone on, but I didn't have the balls enough to do it. I could tell that Bryson knew I was thinking about something because he had his head cocked to the side, staring at me. I could feel the heat going to my face, still not sure what to say.

"What's up?" Bryson asked. I shrugged my shoulders. I felt that if I said anything, I would ruin everything we've gone through. One wrong thing and he could go back to hating me. "Talk to me," Bryson said, but not in a harsh tone.

"What is this?" I asked Bryson, not looking up from the ground. I knew he was still looking at me; I could feel his eyes burning into me.

"What is what?" He asked, seeming genuinely confused. I shrugged my shoulders again. I wasn't one who was big on talking about feelings. Emmy was the only person I could talk to about them, but I hadn't even talked to her about Bryson that much.

"Nevermind, it's stupid." Bryson grabbed my chin, lifting it up so our eyes were meeting.

"Nothing you have to say is stupid, Riley." The way he said my name made my body weak. It was a good thing I was sitting because I probably would have dropped to the ground.

"What's going on with us?" I asked, looking away again. It took Bryson a minute to answer, and I wasn't sure if he was truly thinking about it, or if he was trying to come up with some bullshit answer.

"I don't know, Riley." There he goes again, saying my name that way. "All I know is that I like it. I like that we don't fight anymore." A small smile formed on my lips. "Let's get you to my house before mom and Emmy come looking for us." I chuckled and we headed back to his car.

# Chapter 10

The booming sound of my alarm clock made me want to throw something against the wall; possibly the clock. Fuck, school. I climbed out of bed, slowly grabbing clothes and heading to the bathroom. I took a quick shower and threw on black slim jeans, a black undershirt and a blue plaid button down shirt, rolling the sleeves to my elbows. I ruffled my hair a bit, giving it that messy look, and headed downstairs.

"Good morning, sweetie," my mom said as I plopped down on a stool at the kitchen counter.

"Morning," I mumbled back, still not awake. My mom placed a cup of coffee in front of me. Boy, she knows me so well. I could smell the aroma of bacon filling the kitchen, which made my mouth water. Mmm, bacon. I took a sip of my coffee, burning my mouth in the process.

"Fuck," I yelled, putting my hand over my mouth. My mom shot me a glare; she didn't like vulgar language, and I was pretty good about not swearing in front of her, but sometimes it slipped. "Sorry, mom. That coffee was hot." She chuckled, as if I should have known.

"Bryson? Are you listening to me?" Emmy said. I looked at her, trying to act like I had hear everything she just said.

"Uh huh," I said, looking ahead.

"Then what did I say?" Fuck, she caught me.

"I don't know. I wasn't listening." She rolled her eyes and kept driving.

"Whatever, it's not important. Anyway, I'm making Riley come to the game this Friday." Great, as if I didn't see enough of her as it was.

"Sweet," I said, putting on my best fake smile. Emmy stayed quiet the rest of the ride, which wasn't unusual. We pulled into the school parking lot shortly after, and I dashed out of her car.

"Meet me here after practice," Emmy yelled after me. I shot her a thumbs up and headed to the cafeteria.

Everyone was in their usual seat, around the same table. We had been doing this since freshman year, and it was starting to get old. Everyone knew who the popular kids were; we didn't have to make it even more obvious. But that was the thing with these guys, they wanted everyone to know. They wanted to rub it in everyone's face.

"Yo, Bryson!" Matt yelled as I walked over to the table. I plopped down in my usual seat, next to Tamara. She gave me a smile and kissed me on the cheek. Fuck this fake relationship. I shot her a quick smile before listening in on the groups conversation.

"Seriously though, that dress she was wearing. It was so cute, but it would have looked better on anyone but her,"

Sarah said, rolling her eyes at the end. Who the fuck are they talking about?

"I know," Tamara chimed in. "She thinks she's a hot shot now. I can't wait to ruin that." Tamara laughed, and I could almost guess now who they were talking about.

"She's got brains, but not much more. I mean, maybe if she put a little effort into her hair and makeup, she might actually be pretty," Sarah said. I rolled my eyes at how pathetic they were being. I turned my attention towards the guys, not wanting to hear anymore of the girl talk.

"She was smoking," Matt said. Great, this isn't any better. "I mean, did you see her tits? They're huge!" That got a cheer from the rest of the guys. The bell rang, and I grabbed my bag and headed towards my locker. Matts locker was right beside mine, and he made small talk the whole way. Matt and I had been real close at one point in time, then I found out one of my girlfriends cheated on me, with him, and things just haven't been the same since. "How's that going with Riley?" Matt asked, catching me off guard.

"What?" I asked. I knew what he was talking about, but I didn't want to admit it.

"Is she falling for you yet? Tamara is getting anxious." I rolled my eyes; always about Tamara.

"I think so, but I'm not positive. She's not a bitch anymore, so I've made some progress." Matt chuckled as I closed my locker.

"I can't wait for this all to finish out. I'm surprised Tamara was able to get this all together after that party." I had been so busy actually hanging out with Riley that I forgot Tamara had planned her revenge. Tamara was not someone to mess with. She was practically queen bee of the school, and if you fuck with her, you fuck with all her girls.

"Yeah, it'll be great," I mumbled.

"You don't actually like her, do you?" Matt asked, raising his eyebrows at me.

"Nah, dude. It's just for show." Or was it? I heard someone slam their locker shut, and I looked that way. Fuck, Riley. She must have heard everything I said. Now look at what I got myself into.

Calculus was quiet. Ms. Miller paired Riley and I up for a group activity, but Riley just did all the work and sat there. She wouldn't even look at me. I knew then that she must have heard everything. I sighed, which made Riley look in my direction quickly and then look away. When the bell rang, Riley practically darted out of the classroom.

"Riley," I called, running after her. She stopped, turning to face me with nothing but anger in her eyes.

"What do you want, Bryson?" She was pissed, and I felt bad.

"Will you just talk to me?" She chuckled, stepping closer to me.

"Why? So you can pull me in a little closer and then crush me? Isn't that your plan?" I could see the sadness in her was underneath the anger, and I felt genuinely bad.

"It's not like that," I said, trying to form my thoughts into words.

"You know, Bryson, I thought I liked the nice you, but I think I liked when we hated each other better," and with that, she stormed away, leaving me in the hall with everyone staring at me. Great, what have I done?

# Chapter 11

I fought back the tears as I stormed away from Bryson and the group of people watching. I wasn't sure if I was upset because I had been used, or because I really had feelings for him. I kept walking as the thoughts swam around in my head.

"Riley?" A voice said, catching me off guard. I turned around to see Tamara staring at me with a smirk on her face.

"Leave me alone, Tamara. You got what you wanted." The smirk instantly got wiped off her face. Did she feel bad?

"Can we just talk? I'm sure that's the last thing you want to hear, but I truly want to explain myself." I chuckled. Tamara wanting to explain herself? As if that would ever happen.

"You have two minutes." She nodded and got closer.

"The night at the party, when you kissed Bryson, it crushed me. I know, everyone thinks we have a fake relationship, but I truly do care about him. I was jealous and stupid, and I came up with this plan. Some how I got him to go along with it." I stared at her as she explained.

"So you actually have a heart?" I said, not thinking before the words came out.

"Yes, Riley, I do have a heart. My heart belongs to Bryson. Even though it was all part of the plan, it killed me to see you guys get close. It seemed to me that he was actually enjoying getting close to you." I rolled my eyes at her.

"Yes, after all this, I'm sure he actually enjoyed getting close to me." Her head dropped a little before saying anything.

"It was a stupid plan, and I'm really sorry for what happened. I didn't think this would happen." I started laughing, and she looked at me confused.

"What did you think would happen then? You know, I don't actually care. I heard what you had to say, and now I'm leaving." I walked away as she called after me, but there was no turning back for me.

I collapsed on my bed when I got home. I didn't want to do anything. I laid there, staring at the ceiling when my phone went off. This better not be Bryson. I grabbed my phone out of my pocket, nearly dropping it on my face.

Emmy- where are you?

Riley- home. Swing by?

Emmy- on my way!

I smiled, knowing that Emmy was probably the only person who could get my mind off of what was going on. Why did it bother me so much? I should have known Bryson was just pretending to like me, but there was something about the way he acted that seemed genuine, not forced. I pushed the thoughts out of my head, still mad about the whole situation. He had a lot to do to prove that he actually enjoyed spending time with me.

"You missed it this afternoon," Emmy said, laying across my bed.

"Missed what?" I asked, confused. I had been at school all day.

"Tamara completely ate shit walking to her car. Her heel broke and she practically went face first into the pavement." I bursted out laughing. That girl had it coming to her.

"That must have been after I left." Emmy nodded with an apologetic smile on her face. "What?" I asked, knowing she wanted to say something.

"I know what happened with Bryson and Tamara." I looked at her, not surprised. Everyone probably knew about it. "I'm so mad at him. I can't believe he would do something like that. He was being so nice!" She let out a sigh, sitting up.

"Exactly. That was all part of their plan." I laid back, not really wanting to talk about it.

"Either way, it's not cool. Especially since he did it to my best friend." I sighed, hoping the conversation would change. "Riley, something will be done about this." And that's what I loved about Emmy. She would do anything to keep me safe, and to make sure I was happy. She treated me as if I was family, and that made up for not having one.

The next morning, I crawled out of bed, dreading the day to come. I was sure people were going to talk about it, and that's exactly what they did when I walked down the hallway at school. People were looking at me, and whispering to their friends. I wanted to tell them I didn't care, but deep down, I really did.

Heads turned when I walked into calculus. I heard the whispers and all the rumors that were going around. Every-one thought I slept with Bryson, and that's why Tamara came after me, but that wasn't that case. I was the innocent one in all of this.

"Riley," the all too familiar voice said from beside me. I ignored him, pulling out my supplies for class. "Will you please talk to me?" Again, I ignored him, flipping pages in my book to make it look like I was doing something. I heard him sigh. I quickly looked up to see him at his own seat. Thank god. At this point, I couldn't care less if I ever talked to Bryson again.

Class dragged on, and I was anxiously awaiting the bell to ring. I wanted to get away. I could feel his eyes burning into me throughout the entire class, but I brushed it off. When the bell finally rang, I threw all my books into my bag and darted out of the room. When I got to my locker, I took a deep breath as I struggled to open it. A hand touched my shoulder, making me jump. I turned around to see the last person I wanted to deal with.

"We need to talk," he said, quietly. I turned back towards my locker, shoving my books inside. "Please, just let me explain." I closed my locker, turning around.

"I don't want to talk to you." I tried to push past him, but he kept blocking my way. "Bryson, if you don't get-" and before I could finish my sentence, his lips were on mine. I could feel the butterflies in my stomach starting to flutter around. My thinking started to get fuzzy, and I almost kissed him back, but I was quickly drawn back to reality. I pulled away and pushed him as hard as I could. I walked away, ignoring the looks and whispers of my peers around me. Could this day get any worse?

# Chapter 12



I watched as she walked away from me. Hurt was taking over every part of my body, but what did I expect? I hurt her, and I knew it. Kids were laughing and pointing at me as I stood there. She got farther and farther from me, but I couldn't move.

"What the fuck was that?" Matt asked, pulling me to reality. I shrugged my shoulders, knowing exactly where he was going with that. "You kissed her, dude!" I turned and started walking down the hallway. I'm not in the mood for this. "Bryson, wait up!" Matt yelled as he caught up to me.

"What?" I snapped, feeling the anger building up inside of me. Matt stopped, staring at me. "What do you want?" I asked, more calm then it should have been.

"You care about her, don't you?" I stopped at my locker, turning the combination. "Admit it. You actually like her." I slammed my fist into the locker, making Matt jump a bit.

"So what if I do? What's the problem? She's not Tamara? I know that, and I'm more than happy with that!" And that's when it hit me. Bryson Carter, the football quarterback, liked

Riley Allister. Not only had it hit me, but I had just admitted it to my friend. Someone I knew wouldn't approve.

"She's a nerd." I slammed my locker door. Shoving my books in my bag, I was trying to think of something to say back. Instead, I started walking away.

"You know, Matt. You're just mad that this will be the one girl you can't convince to cheat on me." With that, I walked out of the school.

I sat in the cafe around the corner from the school. Too many things were going through my mind to even think about paying attention in class. Not like I did anyway. I sat there, staring off into space when my phone went off.

Emmy- where are you? I've been looking all over the place for you.

I decided to just ignore it. She would find me sooner or later, and I knew I wasn't going to hear the end of it. My phone started vibrating furiously off the table, indicating I had a phone call.

"I swear, if this is Emmy," I said to myself. I looked at the phone and saw Tamara's name. Great, the last person I want to talk to. But I decided to answer it anyway.

"What do you want, Tamara?" I asked.

"Babe? Where are you?" I sighed.

"Did Emmy ask you to call me?" I heard shuffling noises in the background, but pushed it aside. I didn't care what she was doing.

"No, I just didn't see you at lunch, so I got worried." I laughed, which came out as a snort. Since when did she care?

"Listen, Tamara, I have to go." I hung up the phone without waiting for her reply. I sat there, in deep thought. An idea hit me, and I knew exactly who could help. I pulled up Emmys text and typed a message back.

Bryson- I need your help. Meet me at home after school.

I got up, leaving a tip on the table. I needed this plan to work.

"You're gonna what?" Emmy asked, too excited for her own good.

"You heard me." I wasn't going to repeat myself just because my sister was too shocked to comprehend what I had said.

"Why, Bryson? Why are you doing this?" I sighed, thinking of a good way to answer her question, but I didn't have to. Emmy could read me like a book. "You actually care about her?"

"Don't sound so surprised." I knew I still wasn't sure how I felt about Riley, but I knew I couldn't not have her in my life. Every time we hung out was amazing. It was always new with her, and she always knew what to say.

"I am though. You guys hated each other for the longest time, and all of a sudden you care about her?" She was right, but once we actually started to get to know each other, it was different. I didn't see her as my sisters annoying best friend anymore; she was so much more than that.

"I know. I don't know what to say, Em. I'm confused. I just need to know that I'm not letting something good go. I mean, what if it could be something?" Listen to me; I sound like a hopeless romantic. "It could be something, or it could be nothing, but I'm not going to know unless I try." I saw Emmys eyes lighten up with my words.

"Bryson Carter, I never realized you had such a heart." She smiled and I let out a small chuckle. "Fine, I'll help you, but if you hurt her, I will castrate you." We shook hands to that, and that's when I knew she fully supported me in whatever decision I decided to make.

Riley's POV

"We're going to a party tonight," Emmy said on the other end of the phone. I sighed, hoping I could get out of it.

"I'm not really in the mood, Ems. I'm the laughing stock at school. It won't be any different at the party."

"You need to not let what people think or say get to you. You're a better person than that. It's never bothered you before." Why did Emmy always have to be right?

"You're right."

"I always am!" I could hear the excitement in her voice. It always happened when she got her way. "Wear a nice dress." A nice dress?

"Why? It's a party." I could hear her sigh in the phone.

"Just do it, okay? Don't ever doubt me." She made a kiss noise and hung up. What had I gotten myself into? I set my phone down on the night stand and headed towards the bathroom. I was stopped by Angela who was making her way out of the bathroom.

"Riley, can I talk to you for a moment?" I nodded my head. Things had been alright for me and Angela lately. She wasn't being a royal bitch anymore.

"What's up?" I asked as I set my stuff down.

"I just wanted to apologize for everything. I never meant for any of this to happen. It was just hard for me, taking on someone else's child. It felt wrong at first. I know that this won't make up for what I've done, but I want you to know that I'm here for you whenever you need me." I smiled, and opened my arms to her. She wrapped me in a hug, and I knew she was sincere.

"Thanks, Angela. It means a lot, it really does. I'm going to a party with Emmy tonight, so I have to get ready." She nodded and headed down the stairs.

After having a nice long, hot shower, I felt ready to take on whatever was going to be thrown at me. I had found a blue dress that had tribal patterns on the top with a blue skirt. I wrapped a brown belt around my waist to complete the look. I threw my hair into a bun and applied light makeup.

"Oh my god! Let me get a picture of you!" Angela said as I walked down the stairs. I smiled and did multiple poses for her. She gave me a quick hug before letting me leave. I hopped in my car and drove to Emmys. When I got there, only her car was in the driveway. Bryson must be at the party already. I mentally hit myself for even thinking about him. Emmy was waiting at the door when I walked up.

"You look stunning, darling," she said in her most convincing British accent. I laughed and walked into her house.

"Only one home?" I asked, plopping on the couch.

"Mom and dad went out for dinner." She purposely left Bryson out, probably knowing I didn't want to talk about him. "Ready to get this show on the road?" She asked. I nodded and we headed towards her car. We sat in silence for part of the ride.

"Angela apologized," I said, breaking the silence. I saw Emmys jaw drop in shock.

"You're kidding?" I shook my head. "That's crazy! Did you forgive her?" I shrugged my shoulders.

"I'm not really sure. She seemed sincere about it, so we'll see what happens." We jammed out to the radio for the rest of the ride. I hadn't noticed where we were going until Emmy parked the car.

"Let's go, buttercup," Emmy said with a smile. When I stepped out and noticed what was around me, I gasped. This bitch had tricked me.

"Emmy, what the hell?"

# Chapter 13

"Let's go, buttercup," Emmy said with a smile. When I stepped out and noticed what was around me, I gasped. This bitch had tricked me.

"Emmy, what the hell?" She just smiled as I took in the beauty surrounding me. From the parking lot I could see the top half of the Ferris wheel. The colorful lights that beamed off of it, and the music that surrounded us. We were at the carnival.

"You like?" She asked, holding a big grin on her lips. She made me dress up for the carnival?

"And I had to wear a dress for this why?" She walked over to me, pulling out her phone.

"Selfie!" She said, snapping a picture. "So we can meet cute guys, duh," she said with a wink. Meet cute guys? I'm not about that life. I looked at her, mouth open like I was ready to say something mean, but I quickly shut it, realizing that this could be exactly what I need.

"Well, let's go meet some guys then!" I said. Emmy cheered and wrapped her arm through mine. She dragged me towards the entrance, pulling out money.

"Two tickets please," Emmy said to the young looking guy behind the counter.

"Eight dollars please," he said with a smile. I could tell Emmy was trying to flirt with him, but I wasn't going to stop her. "Here you are. Have a great time, ladies." Emmy flashed him a smile, and I had to drag her away or we would never get inside.

"Where to first?" I asked her. She started listing off things to do, and I agreed to do whatever she wanted. I was just along for the ride.

After an hour of trailing behind Emmy, my feet were killing me. Knowing we were coming to the carnival, I would have worn proper shoes. I was tempted to take my shoes off, but soon ruled that out.

"Over here," Emmy said. She was standing in front of the fun house with a grin on her face.

"You would make me do this, in a dress might I add." She chuckled and pulled me inside. We spent the majority of our time looking at ourselves in all the different mirrors.

"Imagine if I was really this short and plump," she said. I chuckled at her reflection. I could never imagine Emmy being like an Oompa Loompa. She took a picture and flagged me over.

"We spent too much time at those damn mirrors," I said as Emmy pulled me through the door. My breath caught in my throat at the completely dark room. Not what I was expecting. Emmy still had a hold on my arm, which I was very thankful for. "It's too dark in here," I said to Emmy, but she didn't reply, and that was when I realized she wasn't holding my arm anymore. "Emmy?" I cried out, not knowing where to go. A small spotlight came on, pointed at a wall. The wall had a note on it that read "this way". Should I follow it, or should I just turn back? Ah fuck, what could possibly happen? I followed the notes direction and headed into another dark room.

"Riley," I heard Emmys voice from a distance.

"For fucks sake, Emmy, this isn't funny!" She laughed, but I still couldn't figure out where it was coming from. Another spotlight came on and the note read "turn around". I was hesitant to do so, not knowing if Emmy paid someone to dress as a killer clown and scare me. Clowns were my biggest fear. I slowly turned around, but it was too dark. "I don't know what I'm-" and then a spotlight came on. "What the-," but I couldn't finish. In front of me was Bryson Carter, dressed in khaki shorts and a blue and green checked button down. His hair flowed perfectly, and his eyes sparkled from the light hitting them. "Bryson?" I questioned. Someone pinch me. Am I dreaming?

"I'm sorry," he said, he let his head fall a bit and his arms were behind his back. "I'm sorry for everything." All I could do was stare at him. He was perfect. Stop that, he hurt you. "Say something," he said, now looking at me. I walked closer to him, speechless.

"I should hurt you," was all I could manage to say. A small smile appeared on his face and a chuckle escaped his lips.

"I know," was all he said. He pulled his hands out from behind his back, presenting a bouquet of roses. My favorite. "For you." I took them, taking in their beauty.

"Why? Why are you doing all this?" He stepped closer, and I had all I could do not to step back.

"I care about you, Riley. I know it may not seem like it, and I know I fucked up royaly, but I care." I fought the smile that was threatening to show. I looked down at my feet, not knowing what to do. Did I care about him to?

"Bryson, this is so sweet of you, but-"

"But it's not enough," he said, cutting me off. I let out a sigh. Was that what I wanted him to think? In my heart, he had won me over, but in my head, I wasn't convinced.

"How do I know this isn't all part of your plan? Or rather, to fix your plan?" He looked down as I looked at him. He looked defeated, and it hurt me to see him like that.

"I guess I'll just have to prove it to you, won't I?"

"If that's what you want, but I can't promise that it'll work." I felt like a bitch saying it, but it was true. He had a lot of making up to do before I forgave him. "Look, Bryson, this has been really nice, but I have to go." He shoved his hands in his pocket and looked at me.

"I understand," he said. He started to walk past me, but stopped and kissed me on the cheek. "I'm sorry," he whispered in my ear before disappearing into the dark.

"Really?" Emmy squealed as we walked back to her car. "I told him I didn't know if it would work, but it was worth a shot. I hate seeing my two favorite people upset." She wrapped her arm around me. My whole body felt heavy after what happened. Was I making the right choice? "Riley? Are you listening to me?"

"What? Oh, no, sorry." She frowned at me.

"You're thinking about him, aren't you?" I shrugged my shoulders. How could I not think about him? He was perfect. Stop that right now! He hurt you. My mind and my body were totally against each other, and it drained all my energy.

"Can you just take me home?" I mumbled. She nodded and headed to my house. All the lights were off when we pulled in. "Thanks, Emmy, for trying. It's just going to take time," I said, closing the door. All I wanted to do was sleep, but I couldn't stop thinking about Bryson and what he did tonight.

# Chapter 14

I couldn't sleep. All I could do was toss and turn and think about what happened. She hates me. It kept running through my mind. The night kept replaying. What could I have done differently? I wanted nothing more than for her to forgive me. Who am I kidding? She won't. I knew I messed up, and I was stupid to think that Riley would just fall into my arms, forgiving me after humiliating her. As I laid there, staring at the ceiling, my phone went off.

Matt- party tonight. You down?

Yes, that was exactly what I wanted to be doing right now. I glanced at the clock, noting it was eleven. On the bright side, it was Friday, so what harm would it do to go out?

Bryson- sure. Be there soon.

I got out of bed, pulling on a pair of slim fit jeans and threw on a black tee shirt. I grabbed my jacket and keys and headed out the door. I quietly made my way down the stairs, and just as I was about to open the door, the living room light came on.

"Where are you going?" Emmy asked, looking as if she had just woken up.

"Did I wake you?" She shook her head. "I'm going to a party." She sat up, looking at me. I raised my eyebrow at her, wondering why she cared so much.

"Gonna go find another girl to hurt?" Her words stung. It wasn't like Emmy to act like this. She was the one who helped me try to get Riley to forgive me.

"What's gotten into you?" I ask, leaning against the front door. She stood up, walking towards me.

"I don't know if you actually like Riley or not, but you better figure it out. I know how she feels about you, and if you hurt her again, I will castrate you." I stared at my sister in disbelief.

"I-i do like her, Ems. She just needs time. That's what she said. And for the record, I'm not going to hurt another girl; I'm just going to a party to kill time." She nodded at me and headed up the stairs.

"I meant what I said, Bryson. Do not hurt her again. Oh, and have fun." She smiled and went to her room. What the hell just happened?

"This parties lame," I said to Matt, taking a seat on the couch.

"What, dude? No it's not," he whined. Matt was so far gone, he couldn't tell up from down. I hated being around Matt when he was like this. Mainly because he was drunk when he got my girlfriend to cheat on me. That still hit a nerve with me, but I pushed it to the back burner, knowing no one else knew about it.

"I think I'm going to head out," I said, but Matt was already dozing off on the couch. I got up, grabbing another drink.

"Where are you going?" The voice caught me off guard. It was like déjà Vu. Emmy had said those same exact words to me earlier. I turned around and was met with Tamara's famous smirk.

"I don't think that's any of your business." She placed a hand over her heart, acting as if my words actually hurt her.

"Bryson, I thought we were in this together. We're going to take her down." I held my hand up for her to stop talking.

"I'm done with this, Tamara. I don't want to be part of this plan anymore." Tamara's jaw dropped in shock.

"You can't tell me you actually like her. She's a nerd." I turned and walked way. I was not in the mood to deal with her.

The drive was silent. I had the radio turned down and my window cracked, trying to enjoy the night weather. Riley lives down that road, I thought as I drove by. I did a quick U-turn in a strangers driveway and headed down Riley's road. I parked across the street from her house, staring at the dark house. I pulled out my phone, glancing at the time. One. I saw a light turn on in an upstairs window. Is that her? I could see a silhouette in the window, and then it disappeared. I stared at my phone, debating whether or not to text her. I decided it was worth a shot.

Bryson- hey, you awake?

I kept looking at that window. I saw the shadow move again. It has to be her. It wasn't long before my phone was vibrating in my hand.

Riley- yeah, why?

I got out of my car and walked towards that window. I looked back at her message.

Bryson- look out your window.

Soon after sending that text, the curtains were pulled back and I could see Riley's head peeping around the corner. She closed the curtain, and I thought she was just going to ignore me, but the outside light came on, and Riley came out. She was wearing shorts and a tank top.

"What are you doing here?" She asked as she moved closer to me. I shrugged my shoulders. Basically at a loss for words.

"I was driving by and figured I would stop." Her lips turned up into a smile, but quickly dropped back down when she noticed me looking. "Riley, I-" but she cut me off.

"I'm sorry." I was shocked. Why is she saying sorry?

"For what?" I asked, still confused.

"For shutting you out. The other night was really nice, and I had basically forgiven you then. I just didn't want to get hurt again." I moved closer as she looked down. I felt awful for hurting her like I did. When I was close, she looked up at me. All I could do was wrap my arms around her shoulders, pulling her close to me.

"I'm sorry that I was so fucking stupid. I never should have done that to you." She pulled away and smiled. Damn, you could get lost in those blue eyes. It was like staring into the ocean. I was at a loss for words. I don't know what it is about Riley, but I can't think straight when I'm around her. I pushed a strand of loose hair behind her ear and she smiled. "Let me make it up to you. Let me take you on a real date," I said. She nodded and stepped back.

"I'm free friday," she said.

"I have a game, but after?"

"Sounds great. I'll see you then." She turned away and walked back towards her house. Finally, I thought.

# Chapter 15

School flew by in a blink of an eye. I was beyond excited to go to the football game. Deep down, football was my true love. It was something my dad and I use to watch all the time.

"Riley, over here," Emmy called out. She decided that she was going to kidnap me before the football game and find me something to wear for my date with Bryson. Wow, I'm going on a date. That still hadn't clicked in my head. I walked over to Emmy, who was leaning against her car. "Ready to go?" She asked. I nodded in response and hoped in her car.

"I think these would look great on you," Emmy said, hiding up a pair of black skinny jeans. Emmy had a great sense of style, and I was always happy when she picked out my outfits. It was less I had to do.

"What about this shirt?" I asked, hiding up a peach colored, three quarter length sleeve that hit below the butt in the back. Emmy had a big smile on her face as she held the pants up to match.

"This will look great! He's going to regret not wanting to be with you soon," she said with a wink. I laughed, shaking my head at her comment. "I have the perfect pumps to match this!" Emmy got way to excited when it came to fashion. Whether she admitted it or not, I felt like she would go into the fashion industry once she graduated high school.

"Great, we have an outfit. Let's get out of here," I said with a smile. Emmy just chuckled and we headed up to the counter to pay.

"You ladies find everything okay?" The cashier asked. We both nodded with smiles on our face. "This outfit is gorgeous. I hope you're getting it for a special occasion." I laughed. I loved how people could tell what you were going to do based on your outfit.

"She definitely is," Emmy said, handing her credit card over. I hated when Emmy paid for my stuff, but I knew there was no way around it since she had insisted. The cashier bagged up our purchase and we left.

"Let's get food. I'm starving," I said to Emmy. She shook her head, and I frowned at her.

"I'm not sure what Bryson has planned for your date, but if it includes food, he be upset that you won't be able to eat," she said with a laugh. It was true. I was now going to have to suffer through a football game without eating anything.

"There better be food then," I pouted.

"Good evening, everyone! Welcome to the Raptors field. The coin toss will be in about ten minutes. There is a concession stand with amazing food at the end of the bleachers. All proceeds go to new equipment for the football team!" Everyone cheered as the announcer talked. Emmy and I sat in the middle of the bleachers. We had a perfect view of the whole field and both sidelines.

"This game needs to start already. I'm starving," I said, holding my stomach to be dramatic. Emmy laughed.

"You still have a while, sweet cheeks." I hated when she called me that. She had such weird nicknames for people, and that had to be my least favorite. I groaned at the thought of having to sit through this game without anything to eat.

"Alright, ladies and gentlemen, let's give it up for the Raptors!" The crowd went nuts. You could tell who was rooting for what team. Three quarters of the bleachers were filled with green and gold, the Raptors colors, and the other quarter was filled with white and blue, the opposing team. The Raptors busted through the banner that had been set up in front of the entrance and the crowd screamed. Bryson, Matt, and Andrew, the captains, were the first to break through. Not only were they captains, but they were easily the best players on the team. Once Bryson hit our teams side, he turned to look into the bleachers. He smiled when his eyes locked onto mine. I returned the smile.

"Aw, Riley, he saw us," Emmy said. She always got excited to watch her brother play. He could definitely make a career out of football.

"Let's give it up for the Raptors captains! Bryson Carter, Matt Gerard, and Andrew Milling." Once again, the crowd went nuts as the tree guys made their way to the center of the field. I was too focused on watching Bryson that I missed the rest of the announcements. The ref made his way between the Raptors and the opposing team, who I didn't know. I could see the red talking to the guys and them all shake hands. Soon after, the red through the coin into the air.

"Raptors will be receiving the kick," the announcer said.

The buzzer went off at the end of the second quarter signaling half time. The Raptors were ahead by one point. I could feel the tension in the air. Throughout the first half, I could see Bryson tensing up every time the other team scored.

"Is this team good, or are the guys just having a rough time?" I asked Emmy. She looked just as tense as Bryson did.

"I don't think they're on the same page. Bryson looks like he's ready to rio someone's head off." I nodded in agreement. "Go talk to him," Emmy said, catching me off guard. I knew they would be heading into the locker room any minute. I stood up and made my way down the bleachers. I saw Bryson as I stepped down.

"Bryson," I yelled. He turned, looking to see where the voice came from. I waved at him, hoping he had seen me. A smile formed on his face as he ran over.

"Hey," he said.

"Listen, I know it's getting tough out there. I don't know what's going on with your teammates, but none of you seem to be on the same page." He frowned at my words, but I continued anyway. "You need to give the other team a run for their money. Throw a play at them that they haven't seen yet. Catch them off guard, and I'm sure you'll pull ahead." Bryson's eyes widened at my knowledge.

"Since when did you understand football?" He asked.

"A while. Now go in there, talk to your team, and kick some ass!" He wrapped me in a quick hug and ran off towards the locker rooms.

"Well you weren't gone for long," Emmy says as I take my seat next to her.

"I don't think he needed much of a pep talk, just something to get him going." She laughed at me and shook her head.

"Honey, that is a pep talk." I slapped my forehead.

"Thanks," I said, shaking my head at my stupidness. It wasn't long before the boys came running back onto the field, earning a cheer from the crowd.

"Here we go again," Emmy says. I chuckle, sitting back in my seat. The second half started strong. Bryson had thrown some decent passes to his receivers, earning a touchdown only minutes in to the third quarter. By the end of the third quarter, the Raptors were ahead at 27 while the other team still hadn't scored, keeping them at 14. The boys were on fire. They started the fourth quarter with kick off. The other team managed to catch the ball and run twenty-five yards before being tackled.

"First and ten," the announcer says over the speakers. I could see Bryson on the sideline talking to the coach. Once the other team got the ball again, they managed to make it for another first. They really need to get I top of that guy. Once again, the guy got ahold of the ball, dashing down the field. They were now at the tenth yard line. Then the coach did something I never thought he would do. He subbed a guy out and put Bryson in.

"What the fuck is he doing?" Emmy said, practically on the edge of her seat. Bryson's the quarter back, and never plays outside of his position. "He's going to get hurt," Emmy said. She was clearly not happy about the desicion, but me, well I had all the faith in the world that Bryson would be able to pull through. He was going to keep them from getting a touch down. The guys got into their positions. Bryson taking on the guy who seemed unstoppable.

"Hike!" And the boys went for each other. Bryson was on top of that guy. Bryson looked over his shoulder and saw the ball mid throw. Somehow he was able to catch it. Once his feet hit the ground, he was off, heading for the other side of the field. The crowd was screaming and chanting. Bryson had made it over the fifty yard line before being tackled hard into the ground.

"First and ten for the Raptors," the announcer yelled. You could tell who he sided with. The Raptors offensive line came out, Bryson taking his position as quarter back. The clock was now down to the last two minutes of the fourth quarter. Bryson yelled a couple things to his teammates. The ball flew back into his hands. He stood up, searching around for an open player. Matt was waiting down at the end goal with no one on him. Matt waved his hands and finally got Bryson's attention. Bryson threw a flawless pass which connected with matts hands.

"And the Raptors win," the announcer said, causing the crowd to go wild. Emmy and I screamed, jumping up and down.

"Let's go see him," she said, dragging me down the bleachers. He was standing with the coach and a couple of the players when we got to the field. He shot us a smile, said a few words to his mates and headed over in our direction. Emmy wrapped him in a hug. You could tell how much she cared about him. Once he had put her down, he walked over to me.

"Great job," I said, smiling at him. He wrapped his arm around my shoulder and smiled back.

"I couldn't have done it without that little pep talk."

"I told you it was a pep talk," Emmy yelled, causing us to laugh.

"I have to go shower and change. I'll meet you at my house," Bryson said, planting a kiss on my cheek enforce walking away. Emmy came over, looping her arm through mine.

"Now let's go get you spiced up for this date!"

# Chapter 16

I waited anxiously with Emmy in the living room for Bryson to get home. It was almost eight o'clock. Damn, he must take long showers. Just then, Bryson walked into the house.

"Speaking of the devil," I said with a smirk. Bryson smiled, nodding his head at Emmy and I.

"Ready to go?" He asked. I smiled and stood up.

"Details," Emmy mouthed to me before I walked out. Bryson opened the car door for me.

"My lady," he said, causing me to laugh. I got into the car and waited.

"Since when did you become such a gentleman?" I asked with a laugh. Bryson placed a hand over his heart, as if I actually hurt him.

"I've always been a gentleman. I've just never had the right girl to use my skills on," he said with a wink. I rolled my eyes, pretending to be disgusted.

"You're something else," was all I could say. He really was something else. He was different than any guy I had ever met. We had always hated each other, but was that just to cover up our true feelings? "You know what I just thought of?" I said, breaking the silence.

"Hm?" He said as he paid attention to the road.

"If I never would have gone to that party and played that stupid game of spin the bottle, we wouldn't be where we are right now." I know, it sounded stupid and cliche, but it was true.

"Are you sure about that? I mean, what if I was still able to convince you to help me with math? You think we'd be here?" He had a point. We were always forced to spend time together because I was always with Emmy.

"I don't know," I said truthfully. "We had spent so much time together score that party and yet we still hated each other," I said with a sigh.

"You think I hated you? Wait, you hated me?" He said seriously. I wanted to Palm my face at this boy. He was so clueless sometimes.

"You were always such a jerk. I just assumed." He looked over at me and a smile played at his lips.

"You know that assuming things makes an ass out of you and me, right?" Did he really just say that? I actually hit my forehead with my palm because this boy was nuts.

"I'm glad you got one thing out of that biology class." He chuckled.

"Bryson, this place is beautiful," I said as I stared at the Italian restaurant that we were standing in front of. It looked so classy and expensive.

"I couldn't settle for less than the best for you," he said with a smile. He was so cheesy, but it made me blush. Bryson placed his arm out, motioning for me to grab it. I looped my arm through his and he led me into the restaurant. The inside was gorgeous. I would never had expected it to be an Italian restaurant with the chandeliers hanging from the ceiling. We walked over to the hostess. "Reservations for Bryson Carter, please," Bryson said, shooting her his charming smile. She scanned the list and grabbed two menus.

"Right this way," she said, walking away. We followed her to a booth that was towards the back of the restaurant. I sat down, and Bryson scooted in across from me. "Your waitress will be over shortly for your drinks," she said with a smile and then walked away. I scanned over the menu; my mouth watering at everything.

"So what do you think?" Bryson asked. I shrugged my shoulders, setting my menu down.

"I'll let you know after I taste the food." Bryson chuckled as a young girl walked over to us. She couldn't have been older than sixteen.

"Hello, my name is Alexis, and I'll be your waitress tonight. What can I get you for drinks?" I smiled at we politeness.

"I'll have a sprite, please," I said, looking at Bryson.

"I'll have a root beer," he said. She wrote down our drinks and walked away.

"A root beer?" I questioned, raising my eyebrow. In all the years I had known Bryson, I had never seen him drink rootbeer.

"It's the closest thing I could get to an actual beer." I laughed. He was ridiculous, but it was cute. Alexis came back with our drinks, shooting us a smile.

"You guys all set, or do you need another minute?" I looked over the menu one more time.

"I'll have the lobster Alfredo," I said with a smile. Lobster and Alfredo was my favorite, so they must be good together, right?

"And for you?" Alexis asked Bryson after writing down my order.

"I'll have the steak. Medium rare, please." She nodded and walked away.

"Lobster alfredo, huh?" I nodded as a smile formed on my lips.

"That was so good. I'm pretty sure I have a food baby now," I said, placing my hands on my stomach and leaning back.

"You did devour that quite quickly," Bryson said, chuckling. I rolled my eyes, taking a sip from my drink. "You ready to get out of here?" I nodded as he slipped money into the folder with our bill. I scooted out of the booth and stood up.

"I think I need to be rolled out of here," I said with a groan. Bryson chuckled, wrapping his arm around my shoulder. I smiled as we made our way out of the restaurant. Once again, Bryson opened the door for me, and I slid into my seat. I reclined it back as far as it could go.

"You're really that full?" Bryson asked. I nodded.

"Where to next, captain?" I asked. Bryson shook his head at my comment and started the car.

"That's a surprise."

We talked about anything and everything on the car ride. He still hadn't told me where we were going, and I didn't recognize where we were. It was driving me crazy.

"We're here," Bryson said, parking the car. I looked around to see we were in a huge, empty parkinglot.

"Well this is exciting," I said as I got out of the car.

"You haven't seen where we're going yet."

"But you just said we were here," I said with a groan. Bryson chuckled and grabbed my hand, leading me towards one side of the parkinglot. As we got closer to the end, I could hear the sound of water crashing against rocks. "Are we at the beach?" I asked, getting way too excited. Bryson just chuckled, not answering my question. I could finally see the soft sand and the water in the distance.

"Yes, you figured it out; you party pooper." I chuckled at Bryson and ran onto the sand. I could hear Bryson laughing from behind me, but I didn't care. I hadn't been to the beach in years. Finally, Bryson caught up to me.

"Why did we come here?" He raised an eyebrow at me.

"What? Is the beach not romantic enough?" I smiled, shoving him lightly. "I figured we could relive how we met." I looked at him, confused as to what he meant. I had met him along time ago. I think he could tell I was confused. "I meant the party. I guess we didn't really meet there, but close enough, right?" I laughed, looking out at the ocean.

"Well what did you have in mind?" He smirked.

"Let's play a little truth or dare." Was he being serious right now?

"Ah, what the hell. Why not?" He laughed and we sat on the sand. "Who starts?" I asked.

"You want to start?" I nodded. "Alright, shoot."

"Truth or dare?"

"Truth. I'll start off easy," he said with a laugh.

"Why did you hate me so much?" He looked at me, and I could tell he was really thinking about it.

"I never actually hated you, Riley. It was just a show for the guys." I looked at him, wanting to know more. "I had always thought you were cute. I just knew how the guys would be, but now, I don't care because I run that group." I smiled. "Okay, truth or dare?"

"I'll go with dare." Bryson smirked. He probably didn't think I would choose dare.

"I dare you to go skinny dipping in the ocean." I looked at him.

"Are you kidding? It's probably freezing!" He just chuckled.

"You chose dare," he said with a smirk.

"Fine, but only if you do it with me." He smiled and nodded.

"I guess I could do that." We both stood up and walked closer to the water. I unbuttoned my pants, sliding them off of my waist. I was trying not to watch Bryson as he undressed, but I caught glances every now and again. I slid my shirt off. I was now more nervous than ever. I was going to be completely naked in front of the guy I liked. I saw Bryson looking at me, which made me blush.

"Turn the other way," I said, smiling. He was completely dressed at this point, and I had all I could do to just look in his eyes. He smiled and turned around. I slid off my underwear and unhooked my bra, letting it fall to the ground. I looked at Bryson to make sure he wasn't looking, and I darted for the water.

"Not fair," I heard him yell. I was under the water before he got in. The water was freezing. I fought to catch my breath when I came up for air.

"No one said life was fair," I said with a smirk. He swam closer to me, placing his hands on my waist. He pulled me close and I wrapped my legs around him. He placed his forehead against mine, smiling. Without thinking, I inched closer to him until our lips met. I could tell he was shocked at first, but he soon got into the groove and kissed me back. It was passionate and I could feel the fireworks inside my stomach. Nothing had ever felt so right. What a perfect way to end the night.

# Chapter 17

S urprisingly it was easy to wake up on this Monday morning. Usually, I would be dreading getting up; I would constantly hit the snooze button before Angela would have to come drag me out of bed, literally, but today was different. I was quick to hop out of bed when my alarm went off. I felt refreshed and energized for once. It possibly could have been from my date with Bryson on friday.

"Riley, are you up?" Angela yelled from down stairs. I nodded before realizing she could she me. I mentally slapped myself in the face for that.

"I'm up," I yelled back, grabbing clothes and heading towards the bathroom.

"Great, breakfast is waiting," she sang. I chuckled. Angela had been doing really good. She started going to meetings to help with her addiction. She was no longer staying out all night, or bringing random guys home. She was focused on me now, and it honestly felt amazing. I took a quick shower and threw some clothes on. I put light makeup on, and threw my hair into a bun.

"Good morning, sunshine," Angela said as I walked into the kitchen. I sat down at the island and Angela handed me a cup of coffee. "I'm surprised I didn't have to wake you up this morning." I chuckled.

"Me too. I actually feel good." Angela smiled and set a plate of pancakes and bacon in front of me. The aroma made my mouth water, and I had all I could do not to shove it all in my mouth at once, although that's pretty much what I did.

"You're gonna choke on your food one of these days," Angela said with a laugh. I moaned at how delicious the food was in response.

"So how did it go?" Emmy asked, nudging me in the side. I rolled my eyes. This was like the twentieth time she had asked me.

"It was amazing, Em. It really was." She chuckled at my response. She had gotten all the details over text as soon as I had gotten back from my date.

"I'm glad he's finally being nice." I smiled at her. It was true; after all these years, it was nice to finally be on good terms with Bryson. "So, is it official?" I shrugged my shoulders.

"I don't know. He didn't ask me or anything. We just went on a date." I had been asking myself that same question since Friday night. Are we more than just friends? All I knew was that every time I was with him, I got butterflies, and every time he touched me, my skin felt like it was burning where his hand was. I like Bryson. I knew I did, but I wasn't sure if I wanted to tell him. I needed to know that he felt the same.

"I'll see you after class," Emmy said as she broke away from me. I waved and headed off towards my locker. Of course, my locker was on the opposite side of the school from where my first class was. I rounded the last corner that led me to the hallway my locker was located on. My eyes locked onto Tamara and the guy who was standing in front of her. It looked like Bryson, but it was hard to tell from the back. When she saw me, she grabbed the guy by the collar of his shirt and planted her lips on his. When she finally pulled away, I could clearly see that it was Bryson she swapped her spit with. My heart felt like it had shattered into a million pieces.

"Riley," I heard my name, but I took off in the other direction without even going to my locker.

Bryson's POV

"Bryson, over here." I turned around to see who was calling my name. I rolled my eyes when I saw it was Tamara. Her hair was pulled back into a ponytail, and her clothes looked a couple sizes too small for her. Her shirt came just above her belly button, while her skirt barely covered her butt.

"What do you want?" I asked as she leaned against the row of lockers.

"I haven't seen you in a while, and I missed you." She missed me? I knew Tamara all too well to know that she just missed me. She was up to something, but I didn't know what.

"Yeah, that's great," I replied. I really didn't want to be talking to her right now. I turned and started to walk, but she grabbed my arm.

"Don't you miss me, Bry?" I had always hated that nickname. It was too girly for me.

"It would be awesome if you stopped using that nickname. You know how much I hate it." She laughed her annoying, high pitched laugh that made my ears want to bleed.

"You love it. I know you do." She changed her position, and I noticed how much she was trying to push her cleavage out to try and get my attention. It wasn't working. I had seen her naked multiple time, and there was nothing impressive about it. Let's talk about used and abused. I tried to fight the smile that was coming to my face at that thought. "Or else you wouldn't be smiling." I wanted to tell her why I was smiling, but I knew how that would end. I shook my head in disgust.

"I really need to-" but before I could finish my sentence, her lips were against mine. Her tongue was trying to fight it's way into my mouth, and she had a right grip on the collar of my shirt. When she finally pulled away, I turned around, looking to see if I could figure out what made her do it. There she was. Riley was standing at the end of the hall. Her eyes were wide and her jaw dropped. Fuck. "Riley," I yelled out, but it was too late. She was already gone. I turned back to Tamara who had a smirk on her face. "What's your fucking problem?"

"You're mine, and mine only." I punched the locker, making Tamara jump, before taking off down the hall. This was going to be a great day.

Riley's POV

"How could he do that?" I asked Emmy, who seemed more intrigued with her salad. I balled a napkin up and threw it at her face, finally catching her attention.

"What was that for?" I sat up straight, shooting her a death glare.

"Were you listening to anything I said?" She shrugged her shoulders, causing me to groan in frustration.

"You know how I get when I'm hungry. I'm full now, so please, start over." I chucked another napkin at her and chuckled. She was annoying, but she was still my best friend.

"I saw Bryson kissing Tamara," I said, letting out a sigh.

"Are you sure it wasn't Tamara kissing Bryson?" I shrugged my shoulders knowing that she could be right. Tamara had been doing anything she could she make me miserable.

"I guess it could have been." Emmy chuckled, taking another bite of her salad.

"You're taking something that has been hers for a while." I nodded in agreement.

"She always tries to make my life a living hell."

"I know, but don't worry about it too much. If Bryson likes you as much as I think he does then he'll put a stop to it real quick."

"You're the best," I said, blowing her a kiss. Emmy smiled and then her eyes got wide.

"Can we talk?" I knew that voice all too well. I turned around to see Bryson standing behind me. I nodded, grabbing my stuff and following him out of the cafeteria.

"What do you want to talk about?" I asked, leaning back against the wall.

"I know you saw what happened with Tamara back there, and I wanted to tell you that was all her." I nodded.

"I know. I should have known by the way she glared at me when she saw me come around the corner. Bryson smiled, leaning closer to me.

"I promise you, she's nothing to me." I smiled back, and he wrapped his arms around me. I quickly hugged him back as the bell went off.

"I'll see you later?" I asked before heading off to my next class.

"Definitely," he said, shooting me his famous smirk. There really was something about that boy that made me want him more.

# Chapter 18

There she was, standing right in front of me. Her long brown hair was flowing in the wind as she was looking out at the ocean. The white dress she was wearing was swaying in the wind. She was breathtaking. She turned around, a smile forming on her lips as she moved closer to me. I tried to step forward, but I was frozen in my spot. I looked down, and when I looked back up, she was gone.

"Bryson, wake the fuck up!" Emmy yelled, shaking me.

"What the hell, Em? I was in the middle of a fantastic dream," I pouted. She threw a pillow at me and laughed.

"About Riley?" I shrugged my shoulders. It was none of her damn business. Although, that was the first dream I had ever had about Riley.

"Does it matter?" She shrugged her shoulders and walked out of my room. Finally, some peace and quiet.

"Dude, you missed the rager!" Matt said, walking down the hall beside me.

"There was a rager last night? It was Monday." Matt shrugged his shoulders. "I'm surprised you're here if you raged last night."

"My mom is gonna kill me if I skip anymore school. She's sick of having to come down here and talk to the principle." It was true; Matt was notorious for skipping school. We were only allowed so many 'sick days' before it started counting against our grades, but it was a whole different story if you came to one class and decided to ditch the rest.

"If you keep it up, I'll be surprised if you're allowed to graduate." He chuckled as we stopped at his locker.

"I'll be surprised if I graduate." The realization hit me in that moment. Graduation was only a short month away, and that month would go quick. I instantly started thinking about Riley, and how she still had a year left in this shit hole. Was it too late to do something about how I felt?

"Are you going to eat that?" Matt asked as he stared at my pizza.

"No, you can have it." He had grabbed my slice of pizza before I could even finish my sentence. I was too busy thinking about Riley and what the future might bring. Obviously I couldn't talk to my boys about that. I was known for just sleeping around with girls. I wasn't the type to have a serious relationship, even when I was with Tamara.

"You alright? You've barely said anything this whole time." I shrugged my shoulders.

"No offense, Matt, but you're the last person I would talk to about my personal problems." He smirked, knowing I was right. We had just never had the same relationship since I found out he slept with Ashley, my previous girlfriend. Ever since then, I was against relationships. You really couldn't trust anyone but yourself.

"Nah, dude, it's understandable." I chuckled and he just shook his head. "Just know that I'm always here for you. I know we had our shit in the past, but I still want to be your friend." Fuck, this was the first time he's said anything like this to me. After I found out he slept Ashley, we just kind of let the past be. It always lingered in the back of my mind when we hung out, but we had never talked about it.

"That means a lot. It really does." He smiled and the bell rang. We both got up, emptying the remains of our lunch in the trash.

"I'll catch you later," Matt said before heading in the opposite direction. I gave him a quick nod and headed towards my class.

"Em, are you home?" I yelled through the house as I waked in.

"In my room," she yelled back. I dropped my bag in the living room and headed up the stairs. He door was cracked opened, but I knocked anyway. "Since when do you knock?" Emmy asked with a laugh.

"Just figured I'd be respectful." She smiled and patted the bed beside me.

"I think Riley's wearing off on you. Anyway, what's up?" I took in a deep breath and let it out slowly. It was weird talking about my feelings.

"Actually, it's about Riley." Emmys posture straightened up and she looked serious. "Am I wasting my time?" Her eyebrows furrowed into a confused look.

"What do you mean?"

"Is it too late to do something about how I feel? I mean, graduation is a month away. That will fly, and then we'll have the summer, but she'll still have another year left." Emmy sat silent, hopefully thinking of a way to help me

"I think that's something that you have to decide." I hated when she did that. She was going to leave it completely up to me, and I didn't have the slightest idea.

"That's why I'm coming to you, Em. I don't know."

"Okay, well, do you want to be more than friends?" I don't know; did I? "If you do, you have to consider where you're going to college, and how far away you're going to be. Are you willing to do long distance, or would you rather just have fun in college. If you do long distance, can you trust her? Can she trust you?" Emmys questions hit hard. I wasn't sure if I could even trust myself.

"All I know is how I feel about her." A smile tugged at Emmys lips.

"I think you can handle the rest. Maybe you should talk to her. Spend more time with her, and figure out if you guys could have a future together." Could we? It wouldn't be a high school fling anymore. I'm sure Riley didn't just want a short relationship or even just a fling. She was probably looking for something more, something real.

"Thanks, Em. I'll figure it out." She smiled and I headed out to my room. I laid back on my bed and pulled out my phone.

Bryson- what're you doing?

I sat impatiently on my bed, waiting for Riley to text me back. After what felt like hours, but was only a few minutes, she texted back.

Riley- homework :( you?

Bryson- can I come over?

Riley- sure!

Was I making the biggest mistake of my life?

I stood on Riley's front step, waiting for her to answer. So much was going through my mind. I had no idea if I was making the right choice or not, but I wouldn't know if I didn't try. I heard the lock being undone and Riley was standing before me. I shot her a smile and she motioned for me to come in.

"What's up?" She asked as we walked up the stairs to her room.

"I needed to talk to you." I could see her body stiffen, and I knew I had chosen the wrong choice of words. Fuck, I can't do a damn thing right.

"What about?" She asked as she opened the door to her room, plopping down on her bed.

"I like you, a lot. I've been debating for the last few hours whether this was something we should pursue, and I felt selfish making the choice on my own." She chuckled and I could feel my cheeks burning.

"I like you a lot too, Bryson. I'm up for anything." I let out a breath I didn't realize I was holding. She smiled, placing her hand over mine.

"I want to be more than friends, but I didn't know how you felt because of me graduating next month." She shifted uncomfortably on her bed.

"I guess we just have to see where it takes us, right?" She chuckled lightly. I nodded, grabbing her hand in mine.

"As long as you're happy." I could see the blush rising to her cheeks. I smiled at her as she leaned her head on my shoulder.

"So what does this mean?" She asked, looking up at me.

"Well, Riley, do you want to be my girlfriend?" She giggled and nodded. I laughed as she turned a deeper shade of red. I placed a kiss on her forehead. "I probably should get going. I'll see you tomorrow." She smiled and walked me down to the door. I waved and hopped into my car.

All I could do was smile on the way home. Things were finally falling into place, and it felt like a weight had been lifted off my shoulders. I knew that the college thing was going to be hard, but like Riley said, we'll have to see where it takes us. The house was fully lit up when I pulled into the driveway. Everybody must be home. I shut my car off and unlocked the door. Everyone was sitting in the living room eating ice cream.

"You guys couldn't wait for me?" I pouted. My mother laughed, shaking her head.

"There's ice cream in the freezer, dear. Help yourself, and come join us." You always obeyed my mom. If she told you to do something, you better be doing it. My mom seemed like a sweet, caring person on the outside, but if you did her wrong, you would regret it. I grabbed a bowl out of the cabinet and dished some ice cream in. It wasn't very often we had a family night like this. I could hear whispers as I made my way to the living room.

"How do you think he'll take it?"

"I don't know, but we need to tell him."

"Tell me what?" I asked as I sat on the couch next to Emmy. My mother let out a sigh, and I knew that wasn't a good sign. No one said anything, and I was becoming frustrated. "What's going on?" I asked, looking over at Emmy. I could see the tears forming in her eyes.

"Honey, I have cancer." It felt like someone knocked the wind out of me. I could barely breath, and I could feel my chest tightening.

"W-when did y-you find out?" I stuttered, finding it hard to form sentences.

"Yesterday. I hadn't been feeling very well lately, so I went to the doctor. They ran some tests, and they called me." I was holding back the tears that were threatening to escape. "I start chemotherapy next week, and hopefully it will get rid of it." I looked down at my feet, knowing if I made eye contact with my mother I would start crying. "Bryson? Say something."

"I need air," I said and walked out the front door. I sat on the steps, taking deep breaths to calm myself down. It wasn't working. My mother has cancer. It kept repaying in my head. That one sentence. I heard footsteps behind me, but I didn't turn around to see who it was. I could feel the small arms of my sister wrap around my shoulders. She placed a kiss on my cheek and sat down beside me.

"Bryson-"

"She has cancer," I cut her off. I could no longer controls the tears that formed in my eyes. One after another fell down my cheek, and I didn't care.

"I know; it's going to be hard, but we'll get through it." I leaned my head on Emmys shoulder.

"But what if chemo doesn't work? How long will she have?" I could feel Emmys body shaking, and I knew she was doing all she could to keep herself from loosing it.

"I don't know. That's something we'll have to wait to find out." I wrapped my arms around her. She shouldn't have to be strong for all of us. I know that we need to be strong for mom, but she's my sister, and I need to be strong from her. A sob escaped her lips as she finally let herself cry.

"We'll get through this, no matter what the outcome is. We will always have each other."

# Chapter 19

Everything had fallen into place. Bryson was mine; that was hard to swallow. After all these years of hatred and fighting, he's mine. I laid back in my bed, staring at the ceiling. It didn't take long for me to fall asleep, lights on. I was woken by someone shaking me.

"Riley, sweetie, it's time to get up." When I realized who it was, I shot up from my bed and looked at the alarm clock.

"Shit, I forgot to set my alarm again." Angela laughed, shaking her head.

"The lights were on, so I figured you didn't do much of anything last night." I smiled as the memories from last night came flooding back. "What's got you so smiley?" I laughed.

"Bryson asked me out last night. It just seems too good to be true after everything that we've been through." She smiles and wraps me in a tight hug.

"I'm so happy for you! Now, hurry up and get dressed. Your breakfast will get cold." I nodded and she walked out of my room. I knew this was going to be a good day.

On my way to school, all I could think about was Bryson. Did he tell Emmy? What about his friends? Are they going to accept me? What is the rest of the school going to think?

Who am I kidding? I've never cared what people think. I knew that whatever life was going to throw at us, we could get through it. The parking lot was nearly empty when I pulled in. I parked my car and shoved my books into my bag. I threw my bag over my shoulder as I made sure my car was locked. Just as I assumed, there wasn't many people in the school either. I knew I wasn't that early. Usually Emmy would be here by now. After shoving the books I didn't need I to my locker, I pulled out my phone to text Emmy.

Riley- where are you?

I headed towards the cafeteria to find a table. Some kids were standing in line getting breakfast, and I shuddered at the thought of eating the schools breakfast. It never looked appetizing. My phone started vibrating furiously off the table, and I grabbed it seeing a text from Emmy.

Emmy- on my way!

I smiled at my phone. Emmy and I hadn't really hung out since she helped me pick the outfit for my date with Bryson. It wasn't long before Emmy came trotting into the cafeteria with a tired looking Bryson behind her.

"Hello, darling," Emmy said with a smile.

"Hey, stranger." I looked back at Bryson who had taken a seat, but his head was down looking at his feet. What's up with him? I shrugged it off. Maybe he's just tired. Bryson looked up briefly, catching my eyes. He shot me a quick smile, but it didn't reach his eyes. I smiled back. I looked at Emmy who just shrugged her shoulders. She plopped down on the bench next to me.

"So, my mom wants you to come over for dinner tonight," she said with a smile. I saw Bryson tense up at the mention of his mother. Did they have a fight?

"Yeah, of course. I'll head there after school." I returned the smile, but I kept my focus on Bryson. Something was just weird about him. The bell for first block rang, interrupting my thoughts.

"I'll catch you later," Emmy said, waving us off. I got up, grabbing my bag.

"You coming?" I asked Bryson, who was still glued to his hands.

"Huh? Oh, yeah." He stood up, grabbing his bag. We had first block together, so it was nice that he could walk me to class.

"What's wrong?" He snapped his attention away from his feet and looked me at.

"Nothing's wrong. I'm just tired." Once again, I shrugged it off. He probably was just tired.

First block went by extremely slow, and although I loved math, I just wanted today to be over. Bryson hadn't said a word the whole class period, which was weird for him. Then again, I don't know what weird is now that we're dating. Is he just afraid to let everyone know we're together? I kept sneaking glances at Bryson, but he hadn't taken his eyes off of his note book. Hell, he hadn't even written anything down. When the bell rang, everyone basically ran out of the class room; everyone except Bryson and I. I stayed behind as he shoved his things into his bag and finally stood up. We walked out of the classroom and stopped at my locker.

"You sure you're okay? You've been quiet all day." He looked up at me, and I couldn't read the emotion that was in his eyes, but I knew he wasn't tired.

"Yes, Riley, I'm fine," he snapped. I wanted to take a step back, but I just turned into my locker, grabbing my books. I heard Bryson sigh, like he realized he was in the wrong.

"I'm sorry. I'll see you at my house, okay?"

"Yeah," was all I could say. He placed a kiss on my cheek, and I couldn't help but smile. He smiled back, a genuine smile, and headed down the hall. I closed my locker and leaned up against it. Something must really be bothering him.

All together, the day went by way too slow. I was glad that it was almost summer break. The only thing that would ruin it was when Bryson left for school. He hadn't even told me what school he chose. I practically ran to my car and drove to Emmys house. All of the vehicles were in her driveway, which was slightly unusual. Her parents usually didn't get out of work until five. I turned my car off, pulling the key out of the ignition. The door opened before I could knock, and Mrs. C pulled me into a tight hug.

"Hi, sweetie! I'm so glad you could make it." She looked worn out. Her hair was thrown back into a messy ponytail, she had bags under her eyes, and her clothes looked a little baggy.

"I always have time for your amazing dinners." She blushed at my words. She motioned me to head into the kitchen. Emmy was already sitting at the table and Bryson was leaning against the counter. He shit me a smile when he saw me and walked over, planting a kiss on my cheek. He wrapped his arm around my waist and I could help but laugh at the shock written all over momma C's face.

"I knew this would happen eventually!" She squealed, wrapping us both in a hug. I chuckled as she pulled away. I looked over at Emmy to see her gagging herself. I grabbed a napkin off the counter and balled it up, throwing it at her head. I bursted out laughing when it caught her off guard and she nearly fell out of her chair. These were the moments I lived for.

"Dinner is served," momma C said as she placed a dish of lasagna on the table. My mouth watered at the sight. I dished a big piece onto my plate. I noticed Bryson staring at my with his jaw dropped.

"What? I like to eat, okay?" He shook his head and laughed. He had definitely seen me eat this much before. I took a bite from my lasagna and moaned in enjoyment.

"Is it good, dear?" Momma C asked.

"Mhm," I nodded, shoving another mouthful in. Everyone laughed.

"Thanks for helping with the dishes, Riley," Emmy said as we finished up the last of the dishes.

"When don't I help out? This is like my home." Emmy smiled and we put the dishes away.

"Girls, ice cream!" Emmy and I raced over to her mother, each grabbing a bowl and heading towards the living room. I grabbed my and Bryson's bowl and Emmy grabbed one for her and on for her father.

"Thanks, beautiful," Bryson said as I handed him his bowl. I blushed at his words and plopped down next to him. I was happy to see the change in his attitude from earlier, but I still couldn't help but wonder what was wrong. Shortly after, momma C came into the living room, sitting down next to Mr. C.

"Riley, I have some news I would like to share with you since you are part of my family." I nodded. I was worried, but I felt honored to be apart of the family. Did that make things weird with Bryson and I? I could feel Bryson tense up next to me when his mother talked. I wonder if this was what had been bothering him. "I have cancer," she blurted out. If Bryson hadn't been sitting next to me, I would have dropped my bowl on the ground.

"What?" I knew what she had said, but I couldn't believe it.

"It's going to be a long recovery, but the doctors think we caught it in time." Is that why she looked so tired? Her clothes were too baggy? I couldn't retain what she said to me; I was too shocked.

"You know I will do whatever it takes to help you guys out," I finally said. Bryson rubbed my back, seeming more calm than he was a few minutes ago.

"I appreciate that, dear. Like I said, you are a part of this family." I smiled at her words, but I didn't know how much longer I could hold back the tears.

The mood shifted drastically after the bin momma C had dropped. It was hard, but we played bored games to bring the mood up. It worked. I managed to win monopoly, which never happens.

"I should probably get going," I said as I checked the time on my phone. Momma C wrapped me up in a bear hug, and I couldn't help but smile.

"Come back soon. You're always welcome here." I smiled and sent her a nod. She knew I would probably be here tomorrow.

"I'll walk you out," Bryson said as I put my jacket on. I smiled at him, and we walked outside.

"Is that what was bothering you earlier?" I asked as he walked me to my car. I could hear him scuffing his feet, which drove me nuts, but I didn't say anything, knowing he was hurting.

"Yeah, I just didn't know how to take it. I didn't understand why it had to happen to such an amazing woman." I grabbed his arm, pulling him to a stop.

"She's going to pull through this, Bryson, and she's going to be even stronger than she was before. We all are going to be." He smiled and wrapped me in a hug. "You know in here for you." He nodded, and I rested my head against his chest. We sat like that for a little while before I looked up at him. He smiled, placing his lips against mine.

"You're amazing, Riley Allister." I kissed his cheek and got into my car. He waved as I left. I knew this was going to bring Bryson and I closer, as much as u didn't want momma C to have cancer. We were all going to be okay.

# Chapter 20

The weeks had come and gone, and graduation was only a few days away. Bryson and I had been hanging out non-stop, and I was doing everything I could to spend time at Emmys house. Chemo had been working at first, but it seemed like momma C was getting worse as the days went on. It broke my heart to see practically the only motherly figure I've had suffer so much. Bryson had been taking it pretty hard. The worse she got, the more distant he seemed to get.

"Bryson?" I asked as he stared at his lunch. He hadn't said anything the entire lunch block, and it was very unlike him.

"Yeah?" I met my eyes, and I could see the pain he was feeling.

"Are you okay?" He looked back down at his untouched food.

"Just worried, you know?" I knew exactly how he felt. I had gone through it when my father passed. I wouldn't wish that pain on my worst enemy.

"I do." Bryson knew that my father died, but no one really knew what happened. I hated reliving the night, so I never bothered to tell people.

"You know, you can talk to me about it." The death of my father had traumatized me a lot, but I had finally started to get over it. I knew he was in a better place. I hadn't felt the pain like this in a long time.

"I should be saying that to you. It's your mother that's sick." He shrugged his shoulders, scooting closer to me.

"I know, but I also know how much of a mother my mom is to you." I rested my head on his shoulder and he wrapped his arm around my waist. This was the most PDA we had shown in school since we started dating, and I'm still pretty sure half the school hadn't noticed yet.

"It was one day when I got home from school," I started out, thinking back on that night.

"Dad? Angela? Anyone home?" I yelled as I ran into the house. It was unlike my father to be home when I got out of school. He worked late most nights, and I had his days off memorized by heart because that was the only time I got to spend with him. I ran into the kitchen, checking the calendar.

November 15 Leo: 4-12 office Angela: 8- close dinner

They would always write their schedule down so I knew when I needed to fend for myself for dinner. Today would have been one of those days, except dads car was in the driveway.

"Dad?" I yelled again, but got no answer. I walked into the living room, throwing my backpack on the couch. The TV was on, but it was muted, and there was a half full cup of hot coffee, still steaming, on the coffee table. I walked up the stairs and to my dads room. What if someone broke in? I opened the door to my dads room and saw nothing. I sighed, feeling defeated even though I had only checked three rooms in the whole house. I went into my bedroom and the crumpled piece of paper on my bed caught my attention. I walked over, grabbing the ball of paper and flattened it out. A tear rolled down my cheek when I saw my dads handwriting.

Riley,I'm so sorry I haven't been there for you like I should have been. I'm sorry for all the long hours at the office when I should have been at your softball games. I'm sorry for leaving you with a woman who never wanted children. I'm sorry that I didn't keep your best interests in mind. I'm sorry that I was only doing what made me happy, and I wasn't thinking about you. I'm sorry, Riley, for not being the father that you needed. I love you, and I want you to always remember that. Know that I will always be watching you, and you'll always be safe with me.

The tears streamed down my face as I re-read the note. What was he telling me? He had always been a great father. It never really bothered me that he worked late because I knew that he was doing it for us. He had always been able to give me anything and everything that I ever wanted. He was perfect.

"Dad," I yelled, tears running down my cheeks uncontrollably. I ran out of my room, checking the closets, the dinning room, and the bathroom. Nothing. Was he even here? I didn't know what his note meant. Was he just saying sorry, and that he would be around more? The last place to look was the attic. The stairs were already pulled down, which should have thrown a red flag, but being thirteen, I didn't think anything of it. I slowly climbed the rickety stairs that creaked with every step. I looked around the attic when I made it to the top steps and immediately dropped to my knees. There in front of me was my father, hanging from the attic ceiling.

"I thought it was my fault for the longest time. I didn't have anyone to turn to, except for Emmy, but I never told her what actually happened. Angela had gotten into drugs worse after she got the call, and things had never been the same after that." Bryson rubbed my back as a few tears fell from my eyes.

"I'm so sorry, Riley. I had no idea." I shrugged my shoulders.

"It is what it is. You never know what you have until it's gone, and this whole thing is just making me think of every-thing that I'm going to lose again if momma C dies." Bryson pulled me into a hug, placing a kiss on my forehead.

"We'll get through this together, Riley. I promise."

# Chapter 21

We walked into the bright lights of the local hospital. I could smell the sanitation and sickness all in one. It was beyond disgusting. I hated hospitals, but I knew I needed to be her for mom. It was her fifth chemo treatment, but it wasn't helping. She was just getting worse. She was loosing weight everyday; her hair was starting to fall out, and she had no energy to do anything. Dad had taken over cooking and cleaning. He decided to take all of his vacation time at once to be with mom in this time of need. Six whole weeks he would be at home, making sure everything was neat and in place. Making sure that mom didn't have to do a damn thing around the house. I loved my dad for that. You could see how much her cared about my mom. He would do anything just to make her happy, and this was one of those things.

"Emmy, darling, could you get me a glass of water? These treatments always run me dry." My mom had such a sick sense of humor. The nurses were setting her up to the machine that would pump chemicals into her body. I could see the pain in her face every time she had to come to one of these.

"Of course, mom." I headed out of the chemo room and headed down the bright halls towards the cafeteria. A bunch of sick patients were sitting at the tables. These were the patients that could get around and move on their own. The ones that didn't have to stay in a bed all the time. I found the water station and grabbed a cup, filling it to the top with water. On my way back to the room, I thought about what Bryson was doing. He was suppose to come, but he wasn't at the house when we left. I knew that he hated seeing mom in pain. That's probably why he didn't come. I handed my mom the cup of water when I got into the room. She smiled at me and rested back in her chair.

"Mr. Carter, may I speak to you outside?" The doctor said upon entering the room. I looked at my dad.

"Can I come?" I spoke up. I wanted to know what was going on. She was my mother.

"That's fine." My dad and I followed the doctor into the hallway where he held up an X-ray. "Your wife has gone through five chemo therapy sessions, but as you see here, the cancer isn't going down any. The next thing we can try is radiation treatment." They want to pump radiation into my mothers body?

"Isn't radiation just as bad for her?" I blurted out. My dad shot me a glare, and I sent him an apologetic smile. I hadn't meant to say what was on my mind; it just popped out.

"We only use enough radiation to kill off the cancer cells. Not enough to harm your mother. It will, however, drain her energy more. She'll be more tired." I wanted to punch this doctor in the mouth. I knew he was only trying to help, but she's tired enough as it is. She's lost so much weight.

"I need to speak to my wife about it before we make any decisions." The doctor nodded and we went back into my mothers room. The look on her face said she heard everything that was said in the hallway.

"Why couldn't he tell me all that as well?" My mother asked, clearly hurt that she was included.

"Mom, he probably didn't want to worry you anymore. Doesn't it mean more to make that decision with your family?" I said. She nodded in return. I gave her a peck on the cheek which made her smile.

"Where the fuck have you been?" I said to Bryson as he finally walked through the door.

"Out,l was all he said. I stood up from the couch, placing my hands on my hips. I tried to be intimidating, but it never worked to my advantage.

"You should have been there today. We got more news." At that, Bryson turned all his attention to me. I could tell he was hungry for the information I held.

"And?" I sighed, not wanting to be the bearer of bad news.

"Chemo isn't working. The doctor wants to try radiation treatment, but we haven't decided on anything yet." He slumped down on the couch, letting out a deep sigh.

"Shouldn't we try everything before giving up?" I sat down next to him, resting my head on his shoulder. We were all taking this hard, but I think he was taking it the hardest. He had always been a mommy's boy.

"And what if it doesn't work? We're just going to put her through all of that for it to fail? The doctor said it's going to drain her even more. She's not going to have any energy left, and she can't keep loosing weight. It's not healthy."

"But what if it does work?" He was right, but ultimately it was moms decision. She was going to do what she thought was right.

"We can't play with the what ifs. No matter what we do we're gonna question it." He let out a long sigh before standing up.

"You're right. We should let mom decide." I nodded.

"Mom?" I asked, knocking on her door.

"It's open, sweetie." When I walked in, my mother was wearing her long nightgown, carefully tucked under the covers. She had the tv on, but muted.

"Everything okay?" I asked, sitting on the bed next to her.

"Yeah, just tired is all. All his treatment is taking everything out of me. I think the treatment is going to kill me before the cancer does." I shook my head at her sick sense of humor which made her chuckle.

"Have you decided what you're going to do yet?" I noticed she was watching the bachelor. I didn't understand how she watched that show. It was all about one guy making out with a bunch of different girls, and falling in love with more than one girl. Why would you set yourself up for heartbreak like that?

"I don't think I'm going to do the radiation treatment. I mean, look at how bad it is just from chemo. I feel like if the chemo isn't helping, then why put myself through that?" She had a point, but it still broke my heart.

"I get it. We're all here to help you through this." She smiled, pulling me into a hug.

"I know, darling. I know that you and your brother are going to do great things in life." I started tearing up at her words. It's like she knew she was going to die, and I wasn't ready for that. She wiped away the tears that were rolling down my cheeks and placed a kiss on my forehead.

"I don't want you to talk like that, mom." She sent me an apologetic smile as she relaxed back in her bed.

"No matter what, I will always be with you guys." I smiled and stood up. "I love you, sweetheart. Do you mind sending your brother up here?"

"I love you too, mom." I nodded. I couldn't help but cry uncontrollably after that. Why did I feel like she was nearing the end?

# Chapter 22

The curtains were pulled back in my room when I woke up. I must have forgotten to close them. After talking to my mom, I had gone to my room and drifted to sleep rather quickly. I dragged myself out of bed, thankful it was the weekend. I looked out the window, noticing how grey and dreary it was out. I hated when it rained. You could never find a damn thing to do. I slowly made my way out of my room. Lately, it had been my goal to check on mom when I woke up, but today I felt like getting coffee in my system before trying to hold a conversation. Bryson had gone to Riley's last night after talking with mom. I was happy to finally see them together. I had known all along that they liked each other, they were both too stubborn to admit it. Dad was sitting at the table when I walked into the kitchen.

"Morning, dad," I said with a smile, grabbing a mug and pouring coffee into it.

"Hey, kiddo." Something seemed different about my dad. His eyes were puffy and red, and his hair was a mess.

"Everything okay?" I had never seen my dad cry, and the minute I asked, he bursted into tears. I quickly set my mug down and wrapped him in a hug. In that moment, I couldn't figure out why he was crying.

"Your mother- she passed this morning," he managed to get out in between breaths. That's when it hit me. Mom had cancer, and it had taken her from us. I couldn't help the tears rolling down my face at the realization. This wasn't suppose to happen. She was too young; she was too good of a person.

"It's like she knew," I finally said when I calmed down a bit. My dad looked at me, confusion written on his face. "She made sure to talk to me and Bryson last night." He nodded before placing his face in his hands. "We'll get through this, dad." I sat down at the table across from him, sipping on my coffee, still in utter disbelief. "Does Bryson know?" My dad looked at me and shook his head. "I'll call him." I got up from the table and went to my room. I grabbed my phone off the night stand and dialed Bryson's number. He didn't answer, so I called him again. Of course, he didn't answer. I decided to call Riley, knowing she would probably answer, and to my luck, I was right.

"Hello?" She said. I could hear the sleep in her voice. I must have waken her up.

"Did I wake you? I'm sorry."

"No, it's fine, Em. What's up?" I sighed into the phone. I knew how Bryson was going to handle this, which is exactly why I wasn't going to tell him over the phone.

"Is Bryson there?"

"Yeah, he's sleeping."

"Can you wake him up? I need to speak to him." I heard some shuffling in the background and finally, his groggy morning voice came over the phone.

"What the fuck do you want, Emmy? It's eight o'clock."

"You need to come home."

"Why?" I was starting to get pissed off. Bryson was never this difficult to deal with.

"Just fucking do it, okay?" I heard a sigh on his end, along with some shuffling.

"Fine." I hung up the phone and went downstairs to sit with dad.

You could tell that Bryson was mad that I had interrupted him and Riley by the way he slammed the door shut.

"This better be fucking good, Emmy," he said as he came into the kitchen.

"Mom died," I said, deciding to be blunt. His facial expression changed in seconds and he nearly dropped to the floor.

"No, she couldn't have." My dad had gone upstairs to shower before Bryson showed up, but he was now making his way down the stairs.

"She did, Bryson," my dad said.

"No!" Bryson yelled, slamming his fist into the wall. He left a hole, and I knew he'd be feeling that later. I could see the tears running down his cheeks, and I quickly ran over, wrapping him in a hug.

"It's hard on all of us, Bryson, but we'll get through this. He buried his head into my shoulder, letting sobs out. I rubbed his back, trying to comfort him, but I knew it would take more than that.

"Is that why she wanted to talk to us last night?" He said in between sobs.

"I think so," I assured him. "At least we got to say goodbye." I could feel the tears threatening to fall down my cheeks as I watched my brother be in so much pain. I knew he was going to take it hard. He was a mamas boy.

"I think I'm going to be sick," Bryson said as he took off up the stairs. I slouched down in my chair and buried my face in my hands. Why did this have to happen to us?

Bryson had spent most of the afternoon in his room. I hadn't heard so much as a peep out of him since he found out. I knew he needed time to think about everything, but being alone was the last thing he needed. I walked up the steps, knocking on his door.

"Come in," he said, barely loud enough for me to hear him. I walked in, closing the door behind me. I plopped down on the edge of the bed where he was laying, staring up at the ceiling.

"Are you okay?" I asked, knowing it was a stupid question.

"I will be." I placed a kiss on his cheek and he sat up. "I need to go see Riley." I nodded as he grabbed his things.

Bryson's POV

I made my way out of my house. It was way too hard for me to be there knowing that my mother died in her room. Did she go peacefully? Did it hurt? I knew it probably hurt, all the pain she went through from the cancer and treatments. I knew though that she was in a better place now. She would no longer be suffering, and she would still be looking over us. I threw the car in park and got out, shoving my hands in my pockets as I made my way to Riley's door. By now, my dad must have talked to her step mom. They had always been really close, before her father died. I knocked on the door, waiting for someone to answer.

"Bryson, dear, I am so sorry," Angela said as she let me in.

"Thanks, Angela. Is Riley home?" She nodded and pointed up the stairs. I slowly walked up the stairs and into Riley's room, not even bothering to knock.

"Bryson, oh my god, I'm so sorry," Riley said as she wrapped me in a hug. As she looked up at my, I connected my lips to hers. I didn't know if this was what she wanted. I was pretty sure she was still a virgin, but she was the only one who could make me feel better. Her mouth moved in sync with mine as she wrapped her arms around my neck. I kicked the door closed with my foot, trying not to ruin the moment. Once I heard the door shut, I back her up against the bed, until I felt her touch. She fell backwards, pulling me with her.

"I need you, Riley," was all I could say before our lips met again. I started trailing kisses down her jaw and her neck. Her eyes were closed as she enjoyed the moment. She pulled her shirt over her head, exposing her torso. Damn, she's fit. Yeah, we had gone skinny dipping, but it was dark, and I couldn't see her. I ran my hands down her side, feeling every curve from her shoulders to her hips. It wasn't long before she was pulling my shirt over my head and chucking it across the room. She sat up, pulling my face to hers. I kissed her nose as my hands went to her back, unclasping her bra. When she realized what I did, she held her hands over her chest to keep the bra from falling.

"Bryson," she whispered as I pulled her hands away, letting the bra fall down her arms.

"Baby, you're perfect. Don't ever feel self conscious around me." She bit her lip, and I could tell she was nervous as I took in her chest. You would never be able to tell how big her breasts are from what she wears. I laid her back gently on the bed again, unbuttoning her pants. I slid then down her legs and threw them into the growing pile of our clothes. I met her lips with mine, and I could tell she was hungry for me. The way she kissed me back, forcing her tongue into my mouth. It all seemed so natural for her, but I loved it.

"Bryson, I-I'm a virgin," she said, breaking away. I nodded, looking her in the eyes. She pulled me down and once again, our lips met.

"Do you want this? I'm not going to force you to do anything you don't want to do," I whispered in her ear. She was turning me on just by kissing me. She nodded in approval and I kissed down her neck again. "I'm going to make you feel good, Riley. So good." I kissed to her collar bone, grabbing one of her breasts in my hands. I groped it, feeling her nipple grow hard against my palm. I teased the other one with my mouth. Trailing kisses around her breast before taking her nipple in my mouth. I heard a small moan escape her lips as I flicked her nipple with my tongue. Once I knew she was getting hot, I trailed kisses down to her belly button, stopping above her underwear line. She hit her lip again, causing my boner to grow harder. Fuck, that's hot. I kissed up her thigh, and started rubbing her through her underwear.

"Bryson," she moaned out. I slowly pulled her underwear down, but she crossed her legs as I did.

"What's the matter?"

"I'm just nervous," she whispered, and I could tell how aroused she was.

"Don't be," I smiled at her. She uncrossed her legs, and I pulled her underwear down further, before they fell off her feet. I separated her legs, kissing up her thigh again. I slowly started to rub her lips before separating those. For a virgin, she trimmed up a lot. I licked my lips at the sight of her. Naked, on her bed, with me between her legs. I slipped a finger in, feeling how tight she was. I'm not going to last long. I slowly moved my finger in and out, causing her to moan out. Once she was nice and wet, I licked her lips, before slipping my tongue in between them. I flicked her clít with my tongue. She arched her back and pleasure, and I could hear her breathing picking up. I sucked on it, and I could feel her body beginning to twitch.

"Oh my," she moaned out. I slipped a finger in again, sucking on her clít. I knew she was close, but she didn't, and she had no idea what she was in for. I removed my finger and started rubbing her clít fast. The moans were uncontrollable, and I loved it. It didn't take much more before she came on my hand, her whole body twitching with please. "Oh my god, Bryson," she moaned, fairly loud at that. I smiled as I moved up to kiss her.

"Are you ready?" She nodded, she trying to gain control of her breathing. I pulled the foil wrapped out of my pocket, ditching my pants and underwear. Her eyes grew as my erection popped out of my pants.

"You're going to put that in me?" She asked. I chuckled and nodded in response. I slid the condom down my length and got positioned above her.

"If you want me to stop, just say so." She nodded in understanding and I slowly inserted the tip into her. She let out a cry of pain at first as I slowly moved in and out of her. The more I went, the more I could see her body relaxing. Her walls tightened around my dick, and I knew it wouldn't take long. I thrusted in and out of her, going a little faster each time. Riley was gripping the bed sheets so hard her knuckles were turning white. I smiled, knowing she would eventually get pleasure out of this. I thrusted a few more times before I released myself in her. I pulled out and laid next to her on the bed. I could see the tears running down her cheeks, and I pulled her close. I kissed her forehead as my breathing started to slow down. "I love you, Riley." The words just came out, but I knew it was true how I felt about her. She looked up at me and smiled.

"I love you too, Bryson."

# Chapter 23

I woke up the next morning tangled in Bryson's arms. Memories of the previous night came flooding back. A smile crept onto my face; it couldn't have been more perfect. I knew he was in a rough spot, and I was hoping this wasn't just to make him feel better, but with graduation approaching, I couldn't imagine ending the year a better way. Thinking about graduation made me sad. That meant Bryson and I only had two months to spend together before he went off to college, and who knows what would happen then. Would he still want to be with me? Would he find someone better than me? I knew I should wait and see how it all played out, but I couldn't help the thoughts that were running through my head.

"Good morning, beautiful," Bryson said, catching me off guard.

"Morning," I said back, trying not to show how uneasy I was with everything I was thinking about.

"What's wrong?" Crap, he caught me. I shrugged my shoulders at him, not wanting to upset him. He has way too much on his plate right now to be dealing with my negative thoughts. "You can talk to me, you know."

"I know. You just have other things you're dealing with." I felt the bed shift, and soon his arms were wrapped around me.

"I care about you, Riley. No mater what is going on in my life, I'm still here for you." I smiled at his words. I don't know how I never noticed this side of him before. Oh yeah, maybe that's because we were too busy yelling at each other and throwing things at one another.

"I love you," I said, hoping that it wasn't a dream when he said it last night.

"I love you too, more than anything." He placed a soft kiss on my forehead before climbing out of bed. I watched his naked butt as he bent over to grab his clothes. I tried to hold back a chuckle, but I knew he caught it when he sent daggers my way.

"You have a nice butt," I said, still chuckling. He smirked and threw his boxers at me, making me cringe. "Gross, those are dirty," I squealed, throwing them to the floor.

"I'm going to take a shower. Care to join?" He asked, winking at me. I could feel my cheeks heat up. We hadn't really seen each other naked. Both times it was too dark to see anything. I grabbed his shirt from the floor, throwing it over myself before climbing out of bed.

"Sure," I smiled, walking into the bathroom.

Bryson was close behind me, closing the door as he entered the bathroom. I sat on the toilet, watching as he turned the water on. He hadn't bothered to throw any clothing on because he'd just be taking it back off, but me, I was self conscious, even if I could squeeze into a size zero. Bryson walked over to me, and I tried hard to keep eye contact with him, you know, with his thing dangling everywhere. He grabbed my hands, pulling me off the toilet. He started to pull the shirt over my body, but I quickly stopped him.

"Babe, it's okay." I tried to relax my body and just let him do what he wanted. I mean, I couldn't shower in a shirt, could I? Once again, he pulled the shirt over my body, successfully getting it off of me. I tried to cover up, but he pulled my hands away, taking in every inch of my body. "You're beautiful. Stop being so afraid." He kissed me, rubbing his hands down my back. The bathroom was starting to get steamy, and I couldn't tell if it was the shower or because we were both getting into the moment. I parted my lips to get air, and Bryson quickly took advantage of that by sticking his tongue in my mouth. It was weird at first, but it soon felt good. Our tongues fighting each other. He broke away, breathing heavy. He grabbed my hand and pulled me towards the shower. I took in every inch of his body, as he had done to me. Holy shit, was all I could think. He had a thin body with amazing abs coming down to a perfectly defined v. He had a light happy trail leading from his belly button down. His skin was tanned just enough to where he wasn't pale, and every time he moved, his arms flexed into big muscles. We stepped into the shower, the hot water beating down on both of us.

"Well, this is nice," I said. How fucking stupid could you be, Riley? This is nice? Bryson chuckled as he grabbed the loofa and squirted body wash on it. I turned so my back was facing him and instantly relaxed as he started lathering me up with the body wash. He slowly moved down my back, making sure to get my arms. He then rubbed the loofa against my butt, making me jump. His hands began to massage every inch of my back and all the way down to my legs. I would be lying if I said he wasn't turning me on, and the fact that something was poking my lower back, I could tell he was turned on too.

"You're perfect," he whispered into my ear as he rubbed my shoulders. I leaned back against him, relaxing myself. He grabbed the loofa once again, and started rubbing it against my stomach. Once I had enough body wash on me, he used his hands to rub it in. He gently rubbed it into my stomach the moved to my arms. He worked his way up to my collar bone. He slowly moved his hands down to my breasts, rubbing them gently. My nipples instantly got hard at his touch, and I have to admit, it was kind of embarrassing. He managed my breasts before moving his hands back down my stomach. Catching me off guard, he cupped my area, making me jump yet again. He rubbed slowly.

"Bryson," I moaned. I couldn't control what I was feeling inside. The tightening of your muscles when he hits the right spot. He parted my legs and spread my lips, rubbing slowly in between. He placed his finger on my clit, rubbing slowly in circles. Moans were slipping from my mouth, and he knew he was doing a good job. He kissed down my neck as he continued to rub me. I could feel myself ready to go over the edge. He slipped a finger in as he continued to rub me, causing me to cum all over his hand. My back was pressed right against his body as he held me up while I finished. My body was twitching, and it was the best feeling ever. I felt bad that he was the one making me feel good, so I did what I never thought I could do. My back still pressed against him, I moved my hand behind me, grabbing his length. I slowly started pumping back and forth, and I could feel his breathing pick up.

"Fuck, Riley. Keep going." I picked up my speed a little bit faster. He leaned his head against my shoulder as I continued. Being morning and all, it didn't take him long to finish, but I wasn't done. I turned to face him, kissing him quickly. I don't know what got into me, but I started trailing kisses down his neck. I stopped at the bottom of his v and looked up at him. "You don't have to do-," but before he could finish, I was licking his shaft. I knew we were in the shower, but I wanted to make sure it was nice and wet before I put it in my mouth. Once I was content, I slowly put the tip in my mouth. He groaned, placing his hand on the back of my head. Each time, I went a little deeper, trying not to push it too much. I bobbed my head on his shaft. I could feel it pulsating in my mouth. It wasn't long and he came in my mouth, without warning. I swallowed it, not wanting to hurt his feelings. He pulled me up, kissing me. "I love you."

"I love you too."

After our shower, Bryson and I had relaxed a bit before heading to his house. Emmy and their dad wanted to talk about funeral arrangements. It hasn't seemed real until we started planning. I couldn't believe she was gone. After talking about it for a little while, I had lost my cool and bawled my eyes out.

"It'll be okay," Emmy said, wrapping me in a hug. I was apart of the family, and it hit me just as hard. She was the mother figure I never had before, and it hurt to know she was never coming back. After I had calmed down, I noticed that Bryson was gone.

"Where's Bryson?" I asked Emmy. She shrugged her shoulders, so I headed up to his room. He wasn't there, so I went outside, and there he was, standing in the back yard beneath the big oak tree they had. "Are you okay?" I asked as I got closer. Bryson didn't say anything, and all I could do was put my arm around him.

"We planted this tree," he finally said. I looked up at him, hoping he would continue. "I was six, and it was earth day at school. They gave all the students trees to bring home. When I showed her my tree, she pulled me outside and we planted it. Every day during the summer we would take care of it until it was big enough to take care of itself." He couldn't say anymore as he started to cry. I pulled him in, rubbing his back. "I miss her, Riley, and she's never coming back." We stood there in the embrace. I couldn't stand to see him like this. This was the first time I had seen him cry, and I knew he needed me more than ever, so I stood there, hugging him, and letting him get everything out.

# Chapter 24

Today was going to be a hard day. It didn't take much to make me cry as I got dressed. I looked at myself in the mirror. My black skinny jeans stopped at my ankle, met with combat boots. I wore a lacy black tank top, and a blazer over it. I kept reapplying my makeup as the tears came down, smudging it. Eventually, I got frustrated and gave up.

"Riley, honey, you ready?" Angela called up to me. I grabbed my clutch and headed downstairs.

"As ready as I'll ever be," I mumbled, heading out the door. We were meeting the Carter's at the funeral home. I got into the car, slouching in my seat.

"It'll get easier, honey. Just remember, this is a celebration of her life and all the great things she did. After this, it'll be easier."

"Mhm," I said, watching out the window. I could only imagine how Bryson and Emmy were taking this. It didn't take us long to get to the funeral home. We were greeted by Mr. C outside. He gave us both a hug and showed us inside. The room was set up beautifully. They had roses, momma C's favorite flower, everywhere. They had soft music playing in the background along with poster boards of pictures. I could feel the tears building up, and I tried to fight them off. They were having an open casket, and I knew that was going to be the hardest part. When my eyes found momma C's lifeless body laying in the casket, I lost it. I could no longer hold back the tears. Angela wrapped her arms around me.

"We'll be starting shortly," the funeral director said. Angela and I took our seats. They were having the funeral at the funeral home, and from there, the casket would be moved to the cemetery where we would go to watch the burial. I couldn't help but wonder where Bryson and Emmy were. I hadn't seen them since we arrived. My question was soon answered when they both walked in, taking a seat at the front.

The funeral held a lot of tears, but also a lot of laughter of the memories and good times everyone had shared with momma C. Once the funeral was over, Angela and I walked out to the cemetery. We gathered right in front with Emmy. Where's Bryson and Mr. C? Music started playing from the speakers set up outside. Soon, a group of six men came walking out with the casket in hand. As they got closer, I realized that Mr. C and Bryson were right up front, carrying the casket. I could see the tears rolling down Bryson's face, and I knew how hard that must have been for him. Once they got the casket placed where it needed to be, Bryson stood next to me. I wrapped my arm around his waist, and he wrapped his arm around my shoulder. I missed his cheek, hoping he knew I was there for him. He shot me a quick smile before paying attention the the many words that were soon to follow.

"Bryson, this turned out great," I said as I walked over to Bryson. He smiled at me, and I could tell that he calmed down a lot. This was the part where everyone got together to celebrate the good times. Bryson wrapped his arm around me, pulling me close.

"Thank you," Bryson whispered into my ear. I glanced at him, confused as to why he was thanking me.

"For what?"

"For being here for me through everything." I kissed his cheek, and he smiled.

"Is my job. I love you, Bryson, and nothing kills me more than to see you upset."

The night passed rather quickly with a lot of food, dancing, drinking, and laughing. Everyone seemed to be having a good time. I had lost track of Bryson after a little while because he had to go make his rounds to see everyone. I was standing back in the corner by the door, getting tired. A hand grabbed my wrist and pulled me outside. I screamed, but laughed when I saw Bryson. He pushed me back up against the wall, kissing me passionately. When I pulled away, I could smell the alcohol on his breath.

"Are you drunk?" I asked. He just chuckled, pulling me close to him. He nuzzled his head into the nape of my neck.

"Did I tell you how sexy you looked tonight?" He said, slurring his words. I giggled, rubbing his back.

"I should take you home," I said. "Stay put." I went inside to grab the keys from Angela. I quickly told her about Bryson and she laughed, handing me the keys. Bryson was still in the same spot and I dragged him towards the car. I got him buckled up in the front seat and got in the car, driving to his house. It was quite hard trying to carry his dead weight into the house, but I managed to get him to his room. I took off his shoes and got him on to his bed.

"Come here," he said, grabbing my arm. I went to the bed, sitting next to him. He pulled me down, placing his lips on mine. His hand slowly started to move up my tank top, but I pulled back.

"Bryson, you're drunk. You need to sleep." He groaned in frustration, still playing with my shirt.

"But I want you," he said. I shook my head, standing up.

"Not tonight. Go to sleep." He nodded and buried his head into his pillows. I turned the lights off, closing the door quietly. He was asleep before I made it out of the room. I went down the stairs and out to my car. All I could think about was Bryson on my way home. I was thinking about him going to college and leaving me behind. I quickly shook those thoughts out of my head and went to bed right after getting home.

# Chapter 25

"You're literally packing everything in your god damn room," Emmy whined as she laid on my bed, playing on her phone.

"Well, I'm going to be gone for like half a year all together, so I kind of need this stuff." I rolled my eyes. She had no idea what it was like.

"It just looks like you're never coming home," she pouted, finally putting her phone away.

"You know that I'll be back for breaks. It's not like I'm going that far away. It's only an hour and a half." I loved my sister and all, but I was ready to leave.

"How's Riley taking it?" I chuckled, throwing her my phone.

"Look at her messages." She laughed as she read them out loud.

Riley- don't gooooo

Riley- please

Riley- I'm gonna miss you

Riley- you're going to be so far away

"She didn't even let you get a word in," she laughed, throwing my phone back.

"Poor girl. She's going crazy," I said, packing up the last of my stuff.

"She'll still have me," Emmy exclaimed. I zipped up my suitcase, throwing it to the side.

"Yeah, and I'll probably come back more often. I'm going to miss her too." Emmy smiled at my words, pulling me in for a hug.

"Here you go, son. Have fun, and be safe," my dad said after helping me unload my boxes.

"Would you expect any less from me, dad?" He chuckled, giving me a tight hug before leaving. I looked around the room, sighing at all the boxes I had to unpack. I laid on my bed, pulling out my phone.

Bryson- hey you. Made it safe and sound.

Riley had threatened to drive up here and kick my ass if I didn't tell her I made it okay. I know she's worried about not being able to see me much.

Riley- good boy. Be safe okay. I already miss you :(

I missed her more than anything. Besides my family, she was the only one that had been there for me. Yeah, I had gotten condolences from people at school when my mom died, but they weren't my friends; they just felt sorry for me.

Bryson- I miss you too, but it won't be long before you see me again. Have a good day at school, beautiful.

Poor girl still had another year left at that shit show we called a high school. I got up from my bed, deciding to work on unpacking.

"Holy fuck. I have way too much stuff," a voice said, walking into the room. "Hey, you must be Bryson? I'm Charlie, nice to meet you." He held his hand out, and I quickly shook it. I hope he's not crazy.

"Same to you." I opened one of the boxes, groaning at the fact that I hadn't folded my clothes before hand.

"I heard there's a welcoming party tonight. You down to go?" This kid might not be too bad.

"Sure, why not." He smiled and worked on unpacking his boxes.

"This is what they call a party?" I groaned, looking around the room. It looked like the school had set it up.

"Yeah, it looks kind of lame." There were tables set up with drinks and food. Banners were placed above doors saying Welcome Freshman.

"It looks like something you would do for a birthday party, and even at our age it would be lame." He laughed, nodding in agreement.

"There better be alcohol hiding behind around here. I'll be back." Charlie went on his search for alcohol. I stood back against the wall, bored.

"Looks like you need some company," a voice said from beside me. I turned to see a gorgeous blonde standing next to me. Think about Riley. Don't fuck it up.

"Eh, I'm alright." She frowned a bit, looking down at her feet.

"I'm Taylor," she said. It's gonna be hard to get rid of her.

"Bryson," I bluntly said, trying not to seem interested.

"I know where the alcohol is," she whispered in my ear.

"Look, I like to drink, but I'm not looking to get seduced." She chuckled. Why is she laughing? That wasn't suppose to be funny. "I have a girlfriend," I said, hoping she'd get the hint.

"I hope you have a lot of self control," she said, licking her lips. Okay, she's definitely trying to seduce me.

"It was nice talking to you, but I have to go." I quickly walked away, searching around for Charlie, and of course, he was in the kitchen, holding a bottle of beer. "Charlie, I need to go." He raised an eyebrow at me.

"But I just found the beer," he exclaimed.

"Sorry dude, but I'm not all about the drunken whores that just want to get me into their bed." He walked closer to me, eyeing me up and down.

"You have a girl back home?" He asked. I nodded. "She's lucky to have you. Most guys would have let the first girl he saw ride him." I chuckled.

"So we can go?" He nodded and we headed back to the dorm. This is going to be a long year.

# Chapter 26

I couldn't sleep. All I did was toss and turn, and think about Bryson, and how he was enjoying school. I knew I needed to sleep because I started school tomorrow, but I wasn't use to sleeping alone anymore. Bryson had practically lived at my house over the summer. The annoying beeping of my alarm clock pulled me out of my thoughts. I slammed my hand on the snooze button, hoping to get a little sleep.

"Riley, time to get up." Of course. I should have seen that coming. Angela came into my room.

"Do I have to go?" I groaned, really not wanting to do anything.

"Unfortunately, sweetie. It's your senior year. It'll go by quick, I promise." I groaned again, rolling myself out of bed. Screw school.

The halls were filled with students who actually seemed excited to me back. What's wrong with them? I had spent my whole summer with Bryson and Emmy; therefore, I didn't need to beat school to see my friends. I saw Emmy's blonde head bobbing its way down the hallway. She smiled when she reached me.

"Good morning, sweet cheeks." I chuckled. She really had the weirdest names.

"Good morning."

"We have got to have a girls day soon now that Bryson is at college," she exclaimed. I hadn't been taking Bryson's leaving very well. We had spent almost every day together and now, he was just gone.

"That sounds great. I really need to get my mind off things." She smiled.

"Great. Tomorrow after school it is then."

The next day had come and gone in the blink of an eye. My thoughts were still filled with Bryson, whom I hadn't heard much from lately. I knew he had been busy settling in and adjusting to the new place, but it killed me not being able to talk to him. I maneuvered through the sea of kids that were filling the halls. I waved at Emmy when I saw her standing by her car.

"I thought you were going to stand me up," she joked. I chuckled.

"Just got caught in the traffic jam." I got into her car, excited about the shopping spree. Angela had given me money so I could get a new wardrobe for my senior year. Things had definitely gotten better with her. She had been clean for six months; drugs and everything. She had acted more like a mother to me, and it felt nice. After loosing momma C, it felt like I had no one, but Angela quickly stepped in, and she was doing a great job of filling in.

"Oh my god, Riley! Check these gorgeous babies out," Emmy exclaimed. She loved shopping in general, but when it came to shoes, she was lost. She loved her shoes more than anything. Your shoes make the outfit, she had once told me.

"Those are hot, Em!" She smiled, sliding her foot into a tall pair of black heels.

"Well, look who we have here." That voice sounded familiar, but I couldn't place who it was until I turned around. Tamara. I thought she left to college when she graduated, hopefully that was the case, and she was just here visiting.

"What do you want?" Emmy growled. She had hated Tamara from the get go, especially after she had formulated that plan against me.

"Oh, I was just around town and figured I'd come see my two favorite people. Those shoes look a little whore-ish, don't you think?" Emmy's face turned bright red as she bit her lip to hold back whatever she was about to say. Emmy wasn't one to flip out on people, but if they gave her a reason, she would.

"You should probably leave," I finally said, after having an intense stare down with her.

"You're right. I have better things to do. I'll tell Bryson you said hi though!" She winked and walked away. I turned to Emmy, whose face was still red.

"She goes to school with Bryson?" I asked, a little concerned.

"I didn't think so. I thought she was going to California." I nodded, pulling out my phone.

"I guess there's only one person to ask."

Bryson's POV

I had just gotten out of class when my phone vibrated. Riley. I felt bad. I had been ignoring her, but not on purpose. I was trying to get settled in and get ahead with school.

Riley- since when did Tamara go to your school?

I didn't know she had gone to school here. I racked my brain to see if I had seen her around, but I came up with nothing.

Bryson- I didn't know she did, why?

I headed back to my dorm as I waited for Riley to reply. I wish this wasn't the way we were having a conversation after not really talking, but something must have happened to make her text me about it.

Riley- Emmy and I ran into her at the shoe store. She said she would tell you I said hi.

Oh, what the fuck. That bitch could never just leave me alone. She was mad that I had gotten rid of her once and for all. We were in college now. There wasn't the stupid cliques and most popular people dating. I had moved on from that life with Riley.

Bryson- weird. If I see her, I'll straighten it out.

Riley- okay... I miss you.

Bryson- I miss you too, beautiful. I'll be home this weekend though.

Tamara better hope that I didn't see her. She wasn't going to like me after what I have to say. I placed my phone back in my pocket and headed out. She was in for it.

# Chapter 27

I was over the whole wake up and go to school routine. It wasn't even two full weeks into senior year, and I was beyond over the bullshit that came with it. I thought that senior year was going to be fun, filled with adventures, but I was wrong. However, I had one thing to look forward to; Bryson was coming home tonight. I walked down the long hallway of the school, heading for my locker. To my surprise, Emmy was waiting for me. She was the only one that could keep me sane.

"Good morning, beautiful," she said with a smile. Her outgoing personality was contagious, that's for sure. I couldn't help but smile when I was with her.

"You must have me mistaken for someone else," I joked. She chuckled, moving away from my locker so I could get it.

"Bryson comes home tonight," she stated. There was no emotion in her voice whats-so-ever. Had they had a falling out?

"Something wrong with that?" I questioned. Bryson and Emmy had always been close. He was the over protective older brother that would do anything to keep his sister happy, especially after their mother died.

"I haven't heard much from him since he left," she said. I hadn't either, to be completely honest.

"He's just trying to get settled in, that's all." She nodded, and I hoped she believed it. That's all he was doing, right? I closed my locker, walking with Emmy to first period.

With the day being half over, my excitement was building. I couldn't wait to see Bryson. I wanted to wrap my arms around his neck while he wrapped his around my waist, and o could breath in his scent. I never knew you could miss someone so much, and up until he asked me out, I wouldn't have ever thought I would be able to miss him. A smile formed on my face as I reminisced on everything we had been through. If it hadn't have been for that damn math class. I was part way focused on what the teacher was saying when my phone buzzed in my pocket. I carefully pulled it out, looking around to make sure no one was looking.

Bryson- leaving campus shortly. Meet me at my house after school.

I smiled. This was it. He was on his way home, and in just a few short hours, I would be able to hold him. I slid my phone back in my pocket, listening in to what the teacher was saying. Something about the Great Depression in the twenties, but I had other things on my mind. Other things that were making it hard to take in anything the teacher was saying. I stated at the clock, watching as the hands slowly moved. This is going to take forever.

Emmy was waiting by my car when I walked out of the doors to the school. I saw the look on her face, no emotions. What is up with her? I made my way over, preparing myself for the witty comment she was about to make, but she said nothing when I walked up.

"What's up with you?" I asked. She shrugged her shoulders, biting her lip. She only did that when she was nervous, or when she was thinking about a cute boy, but I don't think it's the latter.

"Ready to go see Bryson?" I nodded, feeling the butterflies in my stomach. He still had that effect on me.

"Yeah. He told me to meet him at your house." We got in my car and I quickly put the car in gear to drive to their house. The ride was silent; I didn't know what was up with Emmy, but she definitely wasn't herself. Me. C's car was in the driveway when I pulled in. I hadn't even put the car in park before Emmy was out. I shot her a glare, which she didn't see, and shut the car off. I noticed that Bryson's car wasn't there. Weird. I slowly made my way to the front door, that Emmy had so nicely left open for me.

"Dad?" Emmy called. No response. We walked into the kitchen to see her father sitting at the table. "What's wrong?" She asked, sitting down next to him.

"Bryson was suppose to be here hours ago." I shot Emmy a worried expression, and I could tell that she was just as worried.

"Have you tried calling him?" Her father looked up, and you could tell how stressed he was.

"Of course I have, Emmy." Emmy looked down at the table, not sure of what to say.

"Here, let me try calling to," I finally said. Mr. C shot me a grateful glance as a thanks for breaking that up before it broke into a screaming match. I dialed Bryson's number, hearing his ring back tone.

"Sorry, the number you are trying to reach is currently unavailable. Press one if you would like to leave a message." I hung up the phone.

"No answer," I said as I sat down at the table. Mr. C ran his hand across his face and up through his hair.

"He's never done this before," Emmy said. I looked at her, curious to hear more. "He was excited to come home. Why would he just not show up?"

"Well should call the police," Me. C said.

"They won't do anything until the person has been missing for more than twenty-four hours," I chimed in. They both shot me a glance. "Sorry, I've felt with the police enough." Emmy chuckled, knowing the situation I use to be in.

"What are we suppose to do?" Once again, Mr. C ran his fingers through his hair. I bit my lip, thinking of all the things we could do.

"Emmy and I could go to his school. It's only an hour away." Emmy nodded in agreement as she stood up, grabbing her purse off the table.

"We'll call you if we find anything out, dad." He looked up and smiled.

"Be safe."

Emmy and I spent the hour drive jamming out to loud music to try and get our minds off of what could have happened to Bryson. We didn't want to think worst case scenarios, but that's all that was running through my mind. What if he got mugged, kidnapped? Even worse, what if he got into an accident? I had kept my eyes focused on the road, trying to see if I could catch a glimpse of his car. To my relief, we hadn't seen his car crashed. I pulled into the school parking lot.

"Here we are," Emmy stated.

"Here we are," I said back. I got out of the car and looked around. "Do you see his car?" I asked Emmy. She looked around a bit before shrugging.

"Oh, wait! There it is!" What was he still doing here?

"This boy is going to get a piece of my mind when I find him," I said, making Emmy chuckle. I locked the car, and we slowly made our way to the administration offices.

"Can I help you?" A small blonde said from behind the window.

"We're looking for Bryson Carter's room, please," Emmy said, turning her charm on. She knew we would be lucky if we got it.

"I'm sorry, but I'm not allowed to give that information out." I sighed, thinking it was a hopeless cause. We were going to have to search the whole damn school.

"I'm his sister," Emmy replied.

"Do you have proof of that?" That lady asked. This woman was getting on my nerves. Emmy pulled out her ID and handed it over. "He's in room 312." Emmy gave her a small thank you before we headed to the dorm buildings.

"He better be here," Emmy said. I could tell she was irritated. When we arrived at room 312, I knocked on the door. I couldn't get any movement, but before I knew it, I could hear the deadbolt unlocking and the door opened.

"Yeah?" A tall guy said in a husky voice.

"Is Bryson in?" I asked. His eyes widened, and I wondered if he realized who I was. What other girl would be visiting him, right?

"Um, no. He's uh, out right now," the guy said.

"Well you better tell me where he is. I'm his sister," Emmy finally said.

"Ah, shit. He's uh- he's at a party. Frat house," the guy answered, finally. Emmy and I thanked him and we headed off to the first frat house we found. You could tell there was a party going on. There was blaring music, and people grinding all over each other. Just like they had many times at parties she had gone to. We walked into the house, and Emmy stopped the first person she found.

"Do you know Bryson Carter?" She asked.

"Of course!" The guy said, clearly drunk. "Who doesn't?"

"Well, do you know where he is?" Emmy was definitely irritated. She probably wanted to kill Bryson after this. He could have at least called.

"He was downstairs, in the basement," the guy said, slurring his words. Emmy nodded and pulled me through the crowd towards the basement. We could hear laughter coming from the basement as we made our way down the stairs. It was a whole different scene down here. Different music was play-ing, people weren't grinding on each other, but they were having sex. Awesome. Emmy nudged me, and I looked in the direction she pointed. There Bryson was, half naked on top of some other chick. It couldn't be him, could it? Emmy grabbed my hand, pulling me to her. I could tell by the look in her eyes that it was him. I walked over, giving Emmy one last glance before I stopped in front of these people.

"Bryson?" I asked, trying my hardest not to cry.  He looked up, and when he realized who he was, his eyes grew big. I turned around, storming back to Emmy and dragging her up with stairs.

"Riley, wait!" I heard Bryson yell, but I didn't care. All I wanted was to get out of there. And that's exactly what I did.

# Chapter 28

"R iley, wait!" I heard Bryson yell, but I didn't care. All I wanted was to get out of there. And that's exactly what I did.

I was curled up in my bed with my face in the pillow. Tears were continuously flowing, and I couldn't stop them. What went wrong? He was fine; we were fine. It was all set that he was going to come home this weekend, so what made him go to that party? The image of them, half naked, on top of each other kept playing in my mind. I was never going to un-see that. I thought he had changed.

"Riley?" Angela called as she perked her head in my room. "Emmy's here." I grunted, not wanting to talk. All I wanted was to be alone right now, but I knew Emmy would never let that happen. She always said it's worse when you're alone. The pain will always be worse because that's what you're thinking about. I guess she was right. Emmy came into my room. She didn't say a word; she just wrapped her arms around me, running her fingers through my hair. I was a mess. I couldn't control myself; the tears started to fall harder.

"Sh, it will all be okay." I sat up, looking at her.

"How can you say it will all be okay? The guy that I love was banging some other girl last night, Emmy. That guy that I love is your brother." She sighed, placing her hand on my cheek.

"He will get what he deserves, and he knows it." My phone started vibrating furiously off the night stand, and I groaned.

"Will you break that fucking thing? I'm sick of hearing it." A small smile formed on Emmy's face, and I got help but chuckle at what I had said.

"Is it Bryson?" I nodded in response.

"He's been calling and texting non-stop. I just can't bring myself to look at them." She grabbed my phone, flipping through the messages and voice mails.

"Do you want me to read them to you?" I shrugged my shoulders. I wanted to know what lame excuse he had, but I also wanted to forget about him.

"I'll just read them, I guess." She handed me my phone and I took a deep breath before looking at the messages myself.

Bryson- Riley, I'm sorry. It's not what it looked like.

Bryson- please talk to me.

Bryson- I didn't do it on purpose.

Bryson- Riley, please get ahold of me. I'm worried.

And there were more like that. More messages that would lead to whatever excuse he came up with. I sighed, looking at Emmy.

"You should at least talk to him. See what he has to say, and then you can kick the shit out of him. Hell, I'll even help you," she said in all seriousness. I laughed, and it felt good. It was the first time I could laugh about what had happened.

"I guess I should." I got up, taking my phone into the hall with me, and I dialed Bryson's number. It rang a few times before he picked up.

"Riley? God, I'm so sorry. I'm so s-"

"Shut up," I said bluntly, cutting him off. "We're going to talk about this, but we're going to do it in person."

"Okay. You name the time and place, and I'll be there."

"You have one chance, Bryson. If you don't show up, it's on you. You can forget about me and everything we had." He sighed, and I could hear shuffling in the background.

"I'll be there, Riley. I promise."

"The little dinner in town at noon. That gives you two hours." And then I hung up. I walked back into my room, and Emmy looked at me.

"What happened?"

"I'm meeting him at noon. I told him he had one chance, and if he didn't show then he could forget about me." She nodded and stood up.

"Let me know how it goes." I waited until she left before I started looking for clothes.

It took me an hour to get ready. It was hard. I wasn't looking forward to the conversation that I was about to have. I stepped into the dinner and ordered a coffee before finding a seat towards the back. I sat down and checked the time on my phone. Five of twelve. If he wasn't here by twelve thirty, I was leaving. Soon after, my coffee arrived. I played on my phone and sipped my coffee as I waited. Twelve on the dot and the bell above the door rang. I looked up to see Bryson making his way to my table. He looked like shit. He took the seat across from me.

"Riley-"

"Shut up," I said. I knew I needed to hear his side of the story, but he was going to hear what I had to say first. He stared at me, waiting for me to speak. "I'm just going to get what I have to say out of the way right now."

"Okay," he said, looking down at his hands.

"You're a piece of shit." I could tell he was taken back by my words, but I didn't care. "You have no idea how worried your family and I were last night when you didn't show up. How worried we were when you wouldn't answer our calls. Emmy and I drove all the way to your school, just to make sure you were okay, and you know what we found? You with some whore. You deserve to rot in hell for what you did, and I don't know if I'll ever be able to forgive you. Not just for hurting me, but for hurting your family after everything they've been through." I took a deep breath, trying to calm myself. All Bryson did was stare at me. "Well go on. Now it's your turn."

"I don't know what happened last night." I laughed, and he looked at me like I had two heads.

"You don't know what happened last night? You ended up at a ducking party instead of at home where you were suppose to be."

"I know that," he sighed. "I had time to kill before I left, and my roommate told me about a party, so I decided to go, but things got out of hand..."

# Chapter 29

"I know that," he sighed. "I had time to kill before I left, and my roommate told me about a party, so I decided to go, but things got out of hand..." I could see his face change into one of concentration as he recalled the night before.

Previous night

"Yo, Bryson!" Adam, my roommate, called to me as I finished packing my bag.

"What's up?" I asked. He plopped down on my bed, looking from me to my bag and back again.

"Where are you going?" I sat down next to him, pushing my bag out of the way.

"I'm heading to my house for the weekend." He nodded in response. "What are your plans for the weekend?"

"The usual. Partying and getting laid," he stated. I chuckled.

"Classic Adam thing right there." He smirked, standing up from my bed.

"What time are you leaving?"

"I was planning on leaving at one or two, why?"

"Oh, there's just a party happening as we speak. That's all." I chuckled. He really wanted me to go. "Wanna check it out for a few?" I shrugged.

"Why not? I have time to kill."

It was weird that there was a party happening this early. Everyone had classes, so they would usually schedule the party for after school. Adam and I made our way to the frat house down the hill from the dorms. You could hear the music bumping from down the street. How did we never get in trouble for parties? When we arrived to the house, the party didn't seem spectacular. Since it was day time, there were no crazy lights flashing, and most of the people were hiding inside, probably so they didn't get caught. You could see people going in and out of the house, mainly heading for the backyard.

"What, is this some kind of pool party?" I asked. Adam shrugged, walking into the house. I followed closely behind him. The inside was like every other party I had ever been to. The music was blasting, people were holding red solo cups high above their head as they grinded with someone they probably didn't know.

"I'm going to get a drink. You want one?"

"I'll have a soda. I have to drive, remember?" He nodded and made his way to the kitchen. I stood awkwardly to the side of the room, trying not to get randomly touched by drunken girls.

"Bryson," a familiar voice says. I look to see Tamara walking my way.

"What do you want?" I spit. I was not in the mood to deal with her.

"Adam told me to bring you this," she says, passing me a drink. "He got caught up with a girl." I nodded. Classic Adam.

I took a sip of my soda, noticing the weird after taste it left in my mouth.

"Christ, Tamara, what kind of soda did he get?" I looked down at the brown liquid.

"Coke, I think?" I stuffed my hand in my pocket, pulling out my phone to check the time.  I still had a half hour before I had to leave the school. I wanted to make sure I was home before Riley got out of school. "So how are things going?" Tamara asked, breaking me from my thoughts.

"Fine," I answered.

"Oh, come on. You can't even have a civil conversation with me?" I shot her a glare.

"Actually, Tamara, having a conversation with you is the last thing I want to do. Last time I checked, you tried to make my life a living hell." She rolled her eyes and stormed off. I stood there for a few more minutes before deciding to find Adam. I checked all around the house, and by the time I made it back downstairs, I had started to feel funny. My head was pounding, and my vision was beginning to get blurry. I walked down the stairs to the basement, holding onto the wall as I went down, trying not to fall. I took a quick glance around the room, spotting Adam in the far corner. Before I could make it over to him, someone grabbed my hand.

"You don't look so good," the unfamiliar voice said to me. I shrugged. I couldn't bring myself to say anything. "Let's find you a place to sit down." She grabbed my hand and dragged me over to a couch that was against the basement wall. I sat down, regretting it instantly. My eyes started to droop, and I couldn't tell what was going on around me. Everything went black.

"Bryson?" I heard Riley's voice. I looked up to see her staring at me with wide eyes.

"Riley, wait!" I yelled as she stormed off through go the crowed. I saw my sisters face turning to follow Riley out of the house.

Present day

"You seriously expect me to believe that you were drugged?" I scoffed. I wasn't believing the bullshit story that was coming out of his mouth.

"I think that's what happened," he said, running his fingers through his hair.

"You think? Why was it so easy to pick out who I was then? Huh?"

"The drugs were wearing off," he replied. I stood up, pushing my chair back with a screech. I wasn't going to listen to anymore of this.

"I'm done, Bryson. Go ahead and fuck whoever you'd like because I'm done." I stormed out of the dinner, slamming my car door shut. I chucked my phone across my car. I should have known all along that this was going to happen. He hadn't changed. It was just different when I saw him everyday. Now that he's at college, he has all the freedom in the world, and no on who knows me to fill me in. But this was it; I wasn't going to give into his tempting looks and sweet words anymore.

# Chapter 30

After leaving Bryson in the diner, I called Emmy, filling her in on everything. She scoffed at his excuse. I didn't blame her because I had done the same thing. It just seemed unreal. Why would Tamara drug him? I knew she was pissed at him, but wouldn't she have come after me instead, like she usually did?

The next morning, I fought with myself. Should I get up for school, or should I stay in bed all day? I finally decided on going to school. I knew Angela would give me an ear full if I didn't. I knew she wanted what was best for me, and at this point in time, getting good grades to go to college was best for me.

Nothing seemed to be going in my favor this morning. The hot water tank decided to shit the bed, so I had a full head of messy hair to deal with. Angela wasn't able to make coffee because we apparently ran out. She was running later than usual, so we couldn't have breakfast.

My stomach growled as I made my way out to my car. God help me if my car breaks down. I unlocked the door, sliding into the drivers seat. I slipped the key into the ignition, and my baby started with ease. I sighed in relief as I threw my backpack into the passenger seat and took off down the road.

When I got to school, Emmy was waiting for me by her car. I pulled into the spot next to her, throwing my car in park and getting out. She looked like she hadn't gotten much sleep. She had bags starting to form under her eyes, and that was very unlike Emmy. She would have thrown a fit on any other day.

"Hey," she said. Something was definitely up with her. She didn't give me one of her quirky lines like usual.

"What's up with you?" I asked, concerned for her well being.

"Bryson stopped by the house last night after you left him in the diner."

"Oh boy. Didn't go well I take it?" She shook her head.

"Not at all. My dad and I ganged up on him. Needless to say, he was not a happy camper by the time he left." I chuckled, glad that he was getting what he deserved. "How are you feeling?"

"Alright, I guess, other than the fact that nothing be was going right this morning." I told her everything that happened and all she did was laugh. The bell rang, signaling it was time to go to class, so Emmy and I went our separate ways.

I sat in chemistry, waiting for the teacher to join us. Kids around me were talking in their cliques about the college party they had gone to this weekend. I rolled my eyes, knowing it was probably the same party that I had attended for a brief moment. The teacher came into the room looking a little frazzled. I looked at the clock. It must have been because she was running later than usual.

"So sorry, class! I was in the office getting paperwork done. We're going to have a student teacher for the next few weeks. I would like to introduce you to Matt," she said. When did he come in? I knew exactly who Matt was. Matt was one of Bryson's friends. One of his friends that didn't like me. It didn't matter now though, right? Matt made a short introduction before the teacher told him to pick a seat to watch for a while. The only empty seat was next to me, of course. Matt took his seat, listening to what instructions the teacher had given us. She handed out a worksheet, probably so she could finish whatever paperwork she needed to.

"Well well. Look at you Riley," Matt said. I rolled my eyes, not wanting to deal with his shit. "You've become an attractive young lady." I turned to him, shooting daggers from my eyes.

"It's only been a few months since you've last seen me, Matt. I haven't changed that much." He sighed, scooting a bit closer.

"Why so bitter, sweet cheeks?" I scoffed.

"Sweet cheeks? Really?" He laughed, making the teacher look in our direction. He shot her an apologetic smile before turning back to me.

"Too soon?" I rolled my eyes, looking back down at my paper. "Psst, Riley," matter whispered.

"What?"

"Let me take you out for dinner," he said. I looked at him, furrowing my eyebrows.

"Why?"

"Because I want to get to know you better. I know what happened to you and Bryson. I'm sorry. Let me help you get your mind off of it." I thought about it for a bit. Matt was right. I did have to get my mind off of it, and he wasn't bad looking. He had lost weight since he went off to college. His slim facial features made his blue eyes stand out more, and he had a very nice smile.

"Fine, I will go out to dinner with you." He flashed me a smile.

"Tonight?"

"Sure."

"Great, I'll pick you up at six." With that, he let me finish my worksheet.

"He what!?" Emmy says excitedly.

"He's taking me out for dinner," I repeated.

"He has gotten cute," she said, placing her hand on her cheek.

"Yeah," I say, taking a bite out of my burger.

"You know that he got one of Bryson's girlfriends to cheat on him?" I looked at her, confusion written all over my face. "Not like you'll be doing any cheating." She smirked.

"We'll see how it goes," I state, looking at my food.

"Don't let what Bryson did get to you. There are better guys in this world, and you never know, Matt might just be one of them. College could have changed him." I nodded, setting my burger down.

"You're right." She smiled, nodding.

"I'm always right," I chuckled, throwing a fry at her.

After school, I headed straight home. Angela was still at work, and I figured the hot water tank hadn't been fixed yet. I went to my room, pulling out a nice pair of dark skinny jeans, a pink silk tank top, and a pair of black boots to finish the outfit. I slipped into my clothes and headed downstairs. I flipped through the channels, searching for something to watch to kill the time. I settled on American Horror Story reruns.

I had gotten so caught up in the show that I hadn't realized it was six until I heard a knock on the door. I glanced at the time, silently cursing the amazing show, and flipped the tv off. I grabbed my jacket, opening the door.

"You look beautiful," Matt said, causing me to blush.

"Thanks. You clean up nicely yourself," I said, taking in his gelled up hair, his blue button down shirt and black jeans. He smiled as I walked outside, locking the door behind me.

The drive was short, filled with a lot of small talk so we could get to know each other. Matt was really interesting.

"I hope you don't mind that I'm not just taking you out to dinner," he said. I looked at him with confusion on my face.

"What do you m-" my sentence fell short when I saw the lights of the Ferris wheel. "Oh my god," I said, getting way too excited.

"Someone sounds excited," Matt said, chuckling.

"I love the carnival!" Matt pulled into a parking space, coming around to my side to open the door. I smiled at him as I got out.

"Where to first?" He asked. I shrugged. Everything about the carnival was my favorite.

"How about we go on some of those cheesy rides they have." Matt smiled, holding his elbow out for me. I wrapped my hand through his arm and we made our way to the Tunnel of Doom.

"That was the worst ride ever," I moaned as we got off the Tunnel of Doom. They had very unrealistic "monsters" that popped out at us throughout the ride.

"You're telling me," Matt laughed. He pointed to another building.

"Freak show?" I questioned as I read the sign. "Why not," I said, shrugging my shoulders. We made our way over to the freak show building.

"Five a person, please," the man told us.

"This better be good," I whispered to Matt who only laughed at my comment. He handed the man a ten dollar bill and we entered the building. The hallway was dark, but you could see the light from a room at the end of the hall. When we got closer to the room, there was a sign on the door frame that read "bearded lady". I pointed out the sign to Matt.

We walked into the room, and I had to cover my mouth to contain my laughter. Standing before us was, in fact, a bearded lady. She wore a red dress with a matching head piece. She looked like a twenties casino performer. We didn't stay in this room for very long. The lady wasn't doing much more than brushing her beard.

We made our way down another hallway that led to another room. The sign read "woman with two heads". I chuckled, knowing that it couldn't be real. We walked into the room, and I gasped at how realistic this woman looked. Both heads looks real. They were both talking and reacting to the crowd.

"I bet they're conjoined twins," Matt said. I nodded in agreement.

We spent another twenty minutes or so checking out the rest of the rooms. After the woman with two heads, we saw the worlds smallest girl and then a guy that was tattooed up to his neck, and he had short arms. Then there was the guy with "lobster hands".

"How real do you think they were?" I asked Matt.

"I'm not sure. It looked pretty realistic to me. Either that, or they have a damn good makeup artist," he said, causing me to laugh. "You hungry?" He asked. I nodded and we made our way to the many food stands that surrounded the grounds.

"Can we go on the Ferris wheel before we leave?" I asked, trailing behind Matt. My feet were starting to hurt from walking so much, and I was tired. It was close to eleven o'clock, and I knew the carnival would be closing soon.

"Yeah, let's go there now," he said, walking over to the ticket booth. He got us each a ticket and we went to stand in line. Luckily there wasn't anybody in line. Most people had left earlier. We entered the car and waited as the guy closed our door and hit their button. I was practically leaning over the side of the cat as we were going up. I loved to be able to look over the carnival and see all the lights. Not only that, but you could see the lights from the close by cities. It was definitely a site worth seeing.

When the car came back down to the bottom, Matt and I got out, deciding to call it a night. We thanked the guy for letting us go, and we made our way back to Matt's car. When we got to his car, I propped my feet up on the dash and reclined my seat back as far as it would go.

"Tired?" Matt asked with a laugh, causing me to look at him.

"A little bit," I said, looking out the window as we drive back to my house.

Angela's car was now in the driveway, so Matt had to park on the side of the street. He got out of the car, once again opening the door for me. He walked me to the steps.

"Thank you, for tonight," I said, making eye contact with Matt.

"Not a problem. It was fun, I hope for the both of us," he said with a smile. I nodded, leaning in closer to him.

"It was definitely fun," I said, placing a kiss on his cheek before waving goodbye to him and going inside. I went up to my room, texting Emmy everything that happened. Once I got into my pajamas, I jumped into bed. It didn't take long for sleep to take over after such a great night.

# Chapter 31

A week had passed since Matt had taken me to the carnival. In that time, he had taken me out to dinner twice, and we went to the movies. Needless to say, he's making a damn good impression. Every time I mention Matt to Emmy, she gets all giddy. She was weary about him at first because he use to steal Bryson's girlfriends, but I think she's warmed up to him now.

"Penny for you thoughts?" Emmy asks as she sits down at the table.

"I'm just thinking about this past week. It's been amazing, and it's definitely keeping my mind off of things." She smiled, placing her hand on mine.

"I'm happy for you. You deserve it. Have you heard from Bryson?" She asks, cautiously.

"He tried multiple times to get ahold of me after that day at the diner, but I think he got the hint," I said. Emmy nodded, letting out a sigh.

"I wish he wasn't so fucking stupid," she groaned.

"That makes two of us. We didn't know he was going to be like this. Hell, if I knew, I wouldn't have wasted my time on him in the first place." She chuckled. The bell rang, and that was my sign to head to chemistry.

"Remember, focus on your studies," Emmy said with a wink. I rolled my eyes, heading towards class.

The class was fairly empty. Usually most people were here by now. I took my usual seat, taking out my notebook, pen, and chemistry book. I pulled out my phone, deciding to scroll through Facebook. After that day in the diner with Bryson, I had deleted him and Tamara off of Facebook. I didn't want to see what they were doing, whether it be partying or each other. I shuddered at the thought. As I was scrolling down my newsfeed, something caught my eye.

Matt Eddies is in a relationship

Oh.

I sighed, closing out of Facebook. He should have told me he was seeing someone else. I put my phone away, waiting for class to begin. Before the second bell rang, Matt came strolling into the room lie nothing was wrong. He had to know that I had seen his relationship status. Should I bring it up? He took his normal seat next to me, plopping his books on his desk.

"Good morning," he said with a smile.

"Morning," I mumbled back. I could see the confusion written on his face with my unenthusiastic reply.

"Something wrong?" He asked. I shrugged my shoulders. "You know you can talk to me about it." I glanced at the clock, knowing I still had a few more minutes before the teacher would say anything.

"I saw your relationship status," I said.

"Oh," was all he could say.

"Yeah, oh. You could have at least told me you were seeing someone else." I couldn't even look at him. He was just as bad as Bryson.

"Riley, I can explain."

"I don't want to hear your excuses, Matt. I really enjoyed spending time with you, and look at where that got us." He sighed, moving closer to me.

"Will you just let me explain?" I shrugged. I knew I wasn't going to win. He was going to tell me whether I wanted to hear it or not. "I didn't want you to find out like this." I chuckled, and he looked at me like I had two heads. "I'm not actually in a relationship."

"What?"

"I put that on there because I was hoping you would say yes to me." I stared at him, not knowing how to take what he had just told me.

"That was for me?" He nodded, placing his hand on mine.

"I wasn't expecting you to see it. I know it's stupid to do it before I even ask you, but I just had a feeling. We have been having such a great time, Riley, and I want that to continue." A small smile formed on my lips.

"You don't think it would be weird since your a student teacher?" He shrugged.

"I don't care. I'm only here for another two weeks." I looked into his eyes, and I could see nothing that showed he was lying. I leaned in, placing a soft kiss on his lips. "So is that a yes?" He asked when I finally pulled back.

"Yes, Matt," I said with a smile.

"Oh my god, Riley! Look at you with all them boys," Emmy said, shaking her ass.

"You're so weird," I stated.

"But you loveeeeeeeee me," she sang, holding out the word love. I chuckled.

"Do you think it's wrong?" She raised her eyebrow.

"Dating Matt? No. Bryson fucked you over. He can't expect you to be stuck on him forever." I smiled.

"You're right. It's in the past, and all I can do is move on."

"That's my girl," she said. I pulled out my phone, deciding to text Angela and fill her in.

Riley- so can he come for dinner?

Angela- of course, darling! I can't wait to meet him :)

I smiled as I opened a new text.

Riley- hey you. Dinner at my house tonight?

I looked up at Emmy who nodded in approval. She knew how hard it use to be for me to bring guys home because of the relationship Angela and I had, but now that we were on better terms, I was excited to bring people home to meet her. I was pulled from my thoughts when Matt texted me back.

Matt- wouldn't miss it for the world :)

I nodded at Emmy, letting her know it was going to happen. She smiled, grabbing her bag just in time for the bell to ring.

"Tell me all about it," she gushed. She had always lived romance movies, and I guess my love life was her own personal romance movie that she could help control, so she always made me tell her what happened.

"Angela, is the chicken done yet? He'll be here any minute," I yelled as I straightened out my blue sundress.

"Yes, honey. I just took it out of the oven!" I looked at the clock, knowing Matt would be here shortly. As if he read my mind, the doorbell rang.

"He's here," I yelled to Angela, running to the door. I yanked the door open, and the smile that had been there was no replaced with a scowl.

"You've got to be fucking kidding me."

# Chapter 32

"You've got to be fucking kidding me," I said as I realized who was standing in my doorway. "What do you want?"

"I want to apologize, Riley. You've been ignoring me ever since the diner." I shrugged, looking away. He should know why I was ignoring him. "I'm sorry, Riley. I know I could say it a million times and you probably wouldn't forgive me." I chuckled, realizing that wasn't the right thing to do. "Regardless of what happened that night at the party, I'm still in the wrong. I shouldn't have done what I did."

"I'm glad you're realizing this now. It took you how long?" I scoffed. I was fed up with his bullshit. I didn't care if he actually was drugged, I couldn't forgive him. "You hurt me, Bryson, and you broke my trust. I don't think I'll ever be able to forgive you," I said.

"Riley?" I heard Matt say as he walked up the walkway.

"Seriously Riley?" Bryson said as Matt wrapped his arm around my waist.

"This is who you go to? You know this guy has managed to steal everyone of my girlfriends, just to piss me off, right?" I shrugged, looking up at Matt.

"Bryson, I think it's time for you to go," Matt stated matter of factly.

"What are you, her boyfriend?" Bryson laughed.

"Close enough, so back the fuck off." The humor in Bryson's face disappeared quickly, and I could tell by the way he was clenching his fists that it wasn't going to end well.

"You need to leave," I told Bryson, hoping to stop a fight before it happened. He started walking away and then turned back to face me.

"I hope you have fun with that scumbag, Riley. He's just using you," he said before getting back into his car. I sighed, looking up at Matt.

"You know that's not true, right?" I nodded, placing a kiss on his cheek. I knew that Matt wasn't the bad guy. Bryson was just mad that I was moving on.

"I can't believe Bryson did that," Angela said as she spooned potatoes onto her plate. I pushed my food around with my fork, not really having an appetite.

"I don't think he'll be coming around for a while," Matt said. Before Bryson got brought up, Angela had grilled Matt with questions about his future and what he was doing for school. I could tell that she was thoroughly impressed with his answers. He had his life thought out, and he was making his dreams come true. I knew that she liked him, and I could tell she was happy that I was getting over Bryson.

"Good. I don't want that boy to come around here again," Angela said. "He's a terrible person." I shot Angela a small smile as I finally ate some of my dinner. I had yet to tell Emmy what had happened with Bryson, but I knew she wasn't going to be happy about it. Emmy and Bryson's relationship had gone down the drain after what he did to me. I think it would have been different if Emmy didn't see it with her own eyes, but she did.

"Thanks for dinner, Angela," Matt said as he grabbed his jacket.

"It was so nice to finally meet you. I've heard nothing but good things, and I hope to see you around more often." She gave Matt a hug and went back to cleaning off the table. I walked Matt out to the door.

"Thank you for coming," I said with a smile.

"It was a pleasure, Riley. I really like you, and I want to show you that. This was just another step to show you how much you mean to me." I looked away, hoping to hide the blush that was burning my face, but Matt grabbed my chin, making me look at him. "Goodnight Riley," he said before inching closer to me. I could feel the butterflies fluttering in my stomach the closer he got. I closed my eyes, waiting with anticipation. His soft lips connected with mine, and the butterflies became a zoo. He pulled away, shooting me a smile.

"Good night, Matt," I said as he walked down to his car. I touched my lips, replaying the scene in my head. I smiled at the thought as I watched him drive down the road. I headed back inside to help Angela with the dishes.

"I like him," she said out of the blue.

"I do to," I said, causing her to laugh. When we finished with the dishes, we went into the living room to end the night with a movie.

The next morning, I rolled into school, sitting in my car, waiting for Emmy. I still hadn't told her about last night, but I knew I needed to. If things like this kept happening, I feel that Emmy might just murder Bryson.

"Hey, lady," she said through the crack in my window. I rolled up the window, getting out of my car.

"Hey," I said with a smile.

"How was dinner last night?" She asked.

"Well, it was good after Bryson left." My words caught her by surprise because when I looked back at her, her jaw was dropped.

"Bryson went to your house?" I nodded. "What did he say?" I filled her in on the story, and she was clenching her fists the whole time. Emmy wasn't a violent person, but if you pissed her off, you should be scared. "I can't believe him," she exclaimed.

"I know. Matt handled it great though. I really thought Bryson was going to throw a punch." She shook her head.

"He's going to pay for everything he's done, Riley. I promise." I have her a small smile as we headed to class.

# Chapter 33

The weeks had come and gone, and I hadn't heard another word from Bryson. Luckily, things were going good, and I didn't need Bryson to keep ruining them. I think he finally got it into his thick skull that I wasn't going back to him. Not after everything that he had done to me.

Emmy and I stood in her room, staring at mass amounts of clothes as we tried to decide what we wanted to wear for graduation.

"This is so frustrating," Emmy exclaimed. I chuckled at her, sitting down on her bed.

"We don't have to get all dolled up for graduation, Em. We can wear a simple sun dress." She rolled her eyes, plopping down next to me.

"What kind of statement would that make though? I want to go out with a bang!" I laughed. Emmy was all about making a statement. Especially since we were leaving this shit hole forever, she wanted to make it the most memorable thing in high school.

"Well, you know I'm not one to make statements, so I'm just going to stick to a sun dress," I said, standing up. I started searching through all the dresses that Emmy and I owned.

Yes, I brought all my nice clothes over so we had choices. Neither one of us wanted to spend a bunch of money on a dress just to wear for an hour or so.

"You're so boring," Emmy said, dragging out the word so. I rolled my eyes, still searching through clothes. I gasped when my eyes landed on one of Emmy's old sun dresses.

"Emmy, you have to let me wear this," I said, holding up the dress. The dress had a dark blue top with a long flowy skirt that had swirls on it in white, light blue, and a green-ish. The strap went around the neck and was decorated with beads. A smile formed on her face when she saw it.

"That would look gorgeous on you! It never really fit me right. You can keep it." I smiled, giving her a kick peck on the cheek.

"You're the best."

It felt like hours had gone by when we both finally found a dress. Actually, I think hours had gone by. Emmy had settled on a short aqua colored dress that was decorated with lace. It complimented her tanned skin. Although we still had another two weeks before graduation, we were both satisfied and ready to walk down the aisle. I had decided to stay at Emmy's house for dinner, since it had taken so long to find dresses.

"You girls all set for graduation?" Mr. C asked. We both nodded in agreement as we stuffed our faves with his homemade mac and cheese.

"It took hours, but we got it," I said when I finally swallowed my food. Mr. C chuckled, shaking his head. I went to take another bite of my Mac and cheese when my phone started to vibrate. "Excuse me," I said as I glanced at the unknown number on my phone. Mr. C nodded and I answered my phone. "Hello?" I questioned.

"Hi, honey," the voice breathed out, almost like she couldn't believe she was talking to me. I knew that voice, and it had been a hell of a long time since I last heard it.

"Mom?" I asked, earning looks from both Emmy and Mr. C. They knew the situation with my mom was complicated. I never really talked to her, and I almost liked to keep it that way.

"How are you?" She asked. I could hear the relief in her voice as I talked to her.

"I'm fine. Why are you calling? How did you get my number?" I asked in disbelief. It really had been years since I talked to my mom.

"Angela, but that's beside the point. I wanted to tell you that I'm coming to your graduation." I was uttered speechless. Emmy looked at me with a questioning look as my jaw hung open.

"Why? Why are you trying to be apart of my life now?" Was what I finally spit out when I could finally talk. Emmy knew exactly what was going on now. She was hanging off the edge of her chair.

"Can we talk about this in person, Riley? I would really like a chance to explain." I thought about it for a few minutes. Although I held a lot of anger against my mom, I still hadn't seen her in a long time, and all I wanted was for her to hold me in her arms like she use to.

"Fine," I spit. "Tomorrow after school. Meet me at Angela's."

"I'll see you then," she said. "I love you." I could hear the hesitation in her voice when she said it, almost as if it hurt her to say it.

"Love you too," I said quickly before hanging up. I looked up and Emmy was now the one with the dropped jaw.

"What was that all about?" She asked. I explained the situation as tears rolled down my face. I had so many unanswered questions, and hopefully my mother would be able to answer all of them.

# Chapter 34

Today way the day. The day that I would no longer be a hostage in this hell hole. The day where my real life would begin. The day that I considered becoming an adult. Yeah, I was going to go to college, but it was the time where I was concerned about my future; I knew what I wanted to do with my life, and I was going to school to pursue that dream of mine.

Emmy and I stood in my room, pulling on our dresses, doing each other's makeup, and working on our hair. We still had plenty of time before the actual ceremony, but Mr. C insisted that he take us out to dinner before the big day. Usually when people think about their big day it's a wedding, but for me and Emmy, it was graduation. The both of us were both far from getting married, and this was what was important to us in the moment.

I had yet to hear from my mom on whether she was in town or not. She hadn't gotten a hold of me since the day she called me, but I was still freaking out about what she looked like, how she was doing, and what the hell she was thinking when she left, leaving me with a drug addict step-mother after my father died. Obviously Angela had changed, and I couldn't have been more proud of doing so for my sake. We had an amazing relationship, and it was almost as if she had replaced my mother. Even though Angela and I had our rough patch, she stepped up and took on mothering someone else's daughter. She treated me like her own, and I couldn't be more thankful for that.

"Girls, hurry up. We want pictures before you go to dinner," Angela yelled up the stairs. Emmy and I did the finishing touches before we looked each other over, smiling with approval. We slowly made our way down the stairs, spotting Matt, Angela, and Mr. C waiting for us with smiles on their faces.

"You girls look beautiful," Mr. C said as he gave us both a kiss on the cheek.

"Okay, girls, let's get these pictures done so we can eat," Angela said, clearly excited about the food. Angela took pictures of all of us, then handed the camera off to Mr. C so she could be included in the pictures. Once pictures were done, we all grabbed our bags, ready to head out. I stopped Angela as everyone else left the house.

"Have you heard from my mom?" I asked her. I really was just curious whether my mom was serious about coming or not.

"No, honey, I haven't. Listen, I know it's been a while since you've seen your mom, but don't let it ruin your night if she doesn't come. It might be better off that way." I nodded at her words, knowing that what she was saying was true. Seeing my mom for the first time in years could send me over the edge. I don't know what she'll be like. I looked around, seeing Emmy. Mr. C, and Matt waiting for us at the door.

"We better get going. I think they're waiting," I said, pointing towards their direction. Angela nodded, wrapping her arm around me.

"I have a food baby," Emmy groaned, leaning back in her chair. "If I had pants on, I would unbutton them to have more room." We chuckled at her. We went to Olive Garden, and Emmy thought it would be a great idea to get the endless salad and bread sticks. After about three plates of salad and two bowls of bread sticks, she finally admitted she was full and stopped ordering. It probably had a lot to do with the fact that our server was cute. She just couldn't get enough of him. I wonder if Mr. C noticed her flirting.

"Girls, we better get going if you want to make it on time," Me. C said as he checked his watch. I gathered my clutch and took one last sip of my Sprite before standing up. We all chipped in for the tip since Mr. C insisted on paying for dinner. Emmy hid a ten dollar bill under her cup. I wouldn't be surprised if she wrote her number on it; that's just how she was.

The drive to the school was a short one. Luckily the weather looked like it was going to cooperate, so we would still be able to have an outdoors ceremony. Mr. C pulled up to where the seniors were being dropped off. He gave Emmy a quick kiss on the cheek before wishing us both good luck, and telling us he would be filming the ceremony for us. Angela gave me a big hug, tears already forming in her eyes. I had to walk away before the water works would start for me.

"Here we are," Emmy said as we walked into the cafeteria to kill time.

"Here we are," I repeated, looking around the room at all the seniors in their gap and gowns. Emmy and I quickly got into our gowns, helping each other with pinning our caps on.

"I would say we did it, but I'll save that for when we actually have the diplomas in our hand." I chuckled. We stood around, talking to other classmates as we waited for the final call.

"Okay guys," the principle said. "I just want to congratulate you all in making it this far. I know you're going to hear many speeches tonight, so I figured I would keep this short and just wish you all the best of luck with your futures. Here's to the class of 2015." There were cheers coming from all over the cafeteria. The seniors were pumped up and excited. Too bad the principle didn't know it was because we were all excited to leave this place.

"Split up into your two lines. Make sure you're next to your walking partner," the secretary chimed in once the loudness died down. Emmy was right behind me, due to the fact that no one in our class had a last name starting with B. We would literally be together through the whole thing.

"And now it's time to hand out the diplomas. What do you think class of 2014?" The class erupted in cheers. I grabbed Emmy's hand, knowing we would be the first two to accept our diplomas. Unfortunately, I would still be walking back to my seat as she headed up for her diploma, but I would make due with what I had.

The principle grabbed the first diploma, and Emmy grabbed my hand. I squeezed her hand, shooting her a smile.

"Riley Allister." At the mention of my name, I got up, making my way towards the podium where I would shake hands and finally have my diploma. I shook the secretary's hand, some guy I didn't know, and finally, the principles. "Congratulations," he said with a smile as he shook my hand. He handed my my diploma and moved my tassel to the other side. Once I had my diploma, I turned towards the crowd, holding up my diploma with a smile on my face so Angela and Mr. C could get pictures. People cheered, even though I wasn't their family. It was a day full of excitement. As I headed back to my seat, they called Emmy's name, and I could help but cheer in excitement. I sat down, waiting for Emmy to take her seat again.

When she finally took her seat, she shot me a toothy grin, and I couldn't help but laugh.

Once all the names had been called, the class of 2014 stood up to sing the schools anthem. After we sang the anthem, we threw our caps into the air, waiting for them to come back down. Once they hit the ground, we all scrambled to find our own caps. Emmy threw her arms around me, pulling me in for a tight embrace.

"We did it," she exclaimed. I smiled, nodding at her. Once the room settled down, we made our way over to Angela and Mr. C. Angela have me a tight hug, tears streaming down her face.

"Your father would be so proud of you, sweetheart." And that's when I lost it. Tears started to build in my eyes, and I kept sniffling to hold them back, but that only worked for so long. Matt came over, giving me a hug and a kiss. Angela made us pose for more pictures. I looked around the room, but didn't spot my mother. Maybe she backed out and decided not to come. Who knew, but at this point in time, I didn't care. I was happy that I was surrounded by the people who cared about me. Emmy came strutting over with a big smile on her face. We posed for a couple of pictures. She turned and looked at me.

"We did it," she said, once again. I nodded.

"We did it."

# Chapter 35

I crawled out of bed. Being woken up by loud banging was not the ideal way of waking up. I made my way downstairs, wondering what the hell was going on.

"Angela?" I yelled. I could tell the banging was coming from the backyard, so I headed towards that direction.

"Out here, honey," she called back. I slid the sliding glass door open to see a bunch of men out back.

"What's going on?" I asked as I made my way to Angela.

"Today's your graduation party, remember?" I nodded, but that still didn't answer why these attractive workers were in my backyard. "They're building a picnic table. Mr. Carter and I decided to have the party here since we have a nice sized backyard, but then I realized that I didn't have any where for the guests to sit." I looked at her, still not fully awake. I rubbed my eyes, looking around the yard. One of the younger workers made eye contact with me and shot me a smile that could kill. I looked down to see what I was dressed in: pajama shorts and a tank top with no bra.

"Ah, fuck. I'm going inside before I embarrass myself." Angela chuckled, and I quickly made my way inside. When I got up to my room, my phone was vibrating furiously on the night stand. I picked it up, hitting the answer buttons

"Good morning, sunshine! Are you ready to party today?" Emmy asked, drawing out the word party.

"As long as I don't embarrass myself again, then yes." She chuckled.

"How did you manage to embarrass yourself? It sounds like you just got out of bed."

"I did. Angela hired workers to build a picnic table for the party, and I went downstairs in my pajamas. Let's just say, it was a wee bit chilly out there." I heard Emmy dying of laughter on the other end.

"Let me guess, no bra?" She asked when she finally stopped laughing.

"You got it, and the worst part is, there was a cute one."

"Definitely embarrassing. Whatever, you got a great body. Embrace it!" I sighed at her words, plopping down on my bed.

"I should probably get ready. Knowing my family, they'll start showing up soon."

"I'll be there in like an hour. See ya!" Emmy made a kiss sound before hanging up. I got up, digging through my closet. I pulled out a blue tank top with flowers on it and a pair of light wash shorts to match. I headed into the bathroom to get ready.

"Riley, let's go," Angela yelled into the house.

"I'm coming. I'm just grabbing drinks," I yelled back. Emmy had shown up about an hour ago, and we had just finished setting up when the guests started to arrive.

"Everyone is eager to see you," Angela said as I walked outside.

"I saw them a couple of moths ago. Isn't that enough for them?" Angela chuckled. I had never really gotten along with my dads side of the family. I was just too different. I looked around at the gathering of people and saw the workers from earlier. "What are the workers still doing here?" I asked.

"They worked so hard all morning that I asked them if they would like to stay for lunch." I continued to look around when I saw the worker from this morning.

"Oh god. The cute one is still here. I'm so embarrassed." Angela laughed, shaking her head.

"Honey, I'm sure he's seen plenty of women parts in his time. And he's a young man, he probably enjoyed it." I could feel my face burning up at Angela's words. She was my guardian for Christ sakes. She wasn't suppose to say stuff like that. "Is Matt coming?"!

"No, he had some family stuff to do before he heads back to college."

"It's summer though," she said.

"He's taking summer courses to hopefully finish his degree sooner." She nodded in approval. I knew that Angela like Matt. He treated me well, and that was the most important thing.

"Well, tell him I said good luck. I need to go converse with the rest of the family. Have fun!" She blew me a kiss and wondered off. I made my way over to Emmy to see what she was up to.

"Riley, that guy hasn't taken his eyes off of you since he arrived." I looked over to where she was pointing and saw the cute worker from early, and sure enough, he was still looking at me. I grabbed Emmy's arm and pulled her off to the side.

"That's the worker from earlier that I told you about," I exclaimed.

"Oh, the one that saw your nips?" I covered my ears as soon as the word left her mouth.

"Emmy, you know I hate that word!" She chuckled. I know she just likes to make me uncomfortable.

"You should go talk to him," she bluntly states.

"I'm dating Matt, Emmy, remember?" She shrugs her shoulders.

"Who says you can't make new friends?" I raised my eyebrow at her, but she shoved me towards his direction, and with my luck, he was looking. He shot me another smile, and I rubbed the back of my neck as I made my way over to him.

"Riley, right?"

"Uh, yeah. How did you know?" I questioned.

"Angela told me when she offered us lunch." That sneaky woman. And I thought she liked Matt!

"Oh, right. Uh, about this morning..." I trailed off.

"If it makes you feel better, I can pretend that I didn't see a thing," he said with a smirk.

"That would be great." He laughed.

"I'm Ryker."

"That's an interesting name," I added.

"My parents were a bunch of hippies. That's the best answer I have." I laughed. Angela would probably freak if she knew that.

"Well, Ryker, it was nice meeting you, but I only came over to make my friend happy," I said, pointing in the direction of Emmy, who was not paying attention.

"So you weren't coming to hit on me?" I chuckled nervously.

"Sorry to burst your bubble, but no." He laughed.

"I'm just messing around. Well, before you leave, what would you say to hanging out sometime?" I could feel my face starting to heat up again, and I quickly looked away.

"Uh, yeah, sure. Sounds great!" I told him my number and waved goodbye as I headed back to Emmy.

"So?" She asked when I made it to her.

"He got my number."

"You whore," she joked. I playfully pushed her.

"We better tend to the party. I mean, it is for us after all." She nodded in agreement and we headed off.

# Epilogue

Summer's end was was nearing, and everyone was getting ready for school. I have just finished packing the last of my stuff to make the long drive to North Carolina tomorrow morning.

"Riley, dear, Emmy's here." Emmy decided to go to Paris for school, meaning I wouldn't be able to see her until Christmas break. It was going to be hard. Being in a place where I didn't know anybody. Well, scratch that. I was going to know someone. Matt had transferred schools so he could live with me in North Carolina. Working all summer really paid off. Between the two of us, we had enough to afford an apartment for a couple months, and we were both planning on getting jobs while we're there.

"Coming," I yelled back, shutting the last container and carrying it down the stairs. Emmy was standing by the door with a smile on her face.

"Tomorrow's the big day, huh?" I nodded, setting the box down by the door.

"Shouldn't you be getting ready to get on a plane?" I asked.

"I wanted to stop by and say goodbye." I looked at her and almost burst into tears. "I'm going to miss you so much," she said as she wrapped her arms around me, already crying.

"I'm going to miss you too," I said as the tears began to stream down my face.

"We'll Skype everyday, and it'll be Christmas before you know it," she says, smiling at me.

"Everyday," I say, smiling back. She gave me another hug before saying goodbye to Angela and heading out of the house. I grabbed my last box and headed out the door behind Emmy. She gave a quick wave as she headed down the road. I threw the last box into the truck of my car.

"All packed?" Angela asked as she walked over to me.

"I think so. I hope there is enough room for Matts stuff in here," I said, causing Angela to chuckle. We turned and headed for the door when a car pulled into the driveway. I quickly recognized the car. "I'll be in shortly," I said to Angela, who was going to prepare my last dinner at home for a while. She nodded and headed inside.

"Tomorrow's the day," Ryker said as he walked over to me.

"It is," I said, giving him a hug. Ryker and I had become really close in the short months of summer. He was my go to guy anytime I had problems, besides Emmy that is.

"You're going to keep in touch, right?" He asked, looking me in the eyes. I could feel the blush working its way to my face, and I quickly looked away.

"Of course." He smiled.

"Everyone I know is leaving," he said with a pout.

"We're all a phone call away. Plus, I'm not that far away. You can always visit." He chuckled.

"True. I just wanted to say goodbye before you headed off."

"That's nice," I said with a smile. He moved a little closer, pulling me in for another hug.

"You know, there's one thing I want to do before you leave," he said, no longer making eye contact.

"What's that?" I asked, completely clueless.

"This," he said, before leaning in close and pressing his soft lips against mine. I gasped, taking a step back.

"Ryker..." But he threw his hand up before I could finish.

"I know you have a boyfriend, but I guess that was just my way of showing you how much I've enjoyed the last few months. You don't have to say anything, Riley." I looked at him, surprise written all over my face. "I'm going to go now. Have a safe trip, okay? And don't forget to let me know that you made it safe." Before I could say  anything, Ryker was in his car and driving down the road. I touched my lips were his soft lips were, and it almost felt like butterflies in my stomach when I thought about it. I shook my head, getting rid of those thoughts. Matt would be here any minute to load his stuff in my car and have dinner. I looked down the road that Ryker drove down one last time before heading into the house.

"Riley, will you grab the garlic bread out of the oven?" Angela asked as she set up the table. I walked into the kitchen, grabbing the oven mits and pulled the garlic bread out, setting it on top to let them cool down.

"They're on the stove," I yelled back, grabbing myself a glass of water before heading into the dinning room. Matt and Angela had been cooking dinner because it was my last dinner at home for a while. Even though Matt was going with me, he felt the need to help Angela make the day all about me. I plopped down in my seat at the table, waiting for Angela to serve lasagne. She brought the last of the food in, setting it on the table. I could feel my stomach growl at all the food. Finally, Angela say down and I grabbed the pan, trying to get he biggest piece.

"Hold on, darling. I want to say something before we dig in." I pouted and she laughed. "Over the years I have watched you grow into a beautiful young woman." I rolled my eyes, knowing where this was going. "I know we didn't always see eye to eye, but I'm so glad we have the relationship that we do now. I couldn't be more proud of you, Riley, and the person you've become. I hope you have a great time at college, and I know you have an amazing guy looking out for you." She lifted her glass of wine into the air as well as Matt. I looked down at my glass of water and shrugged my shoulders.

"Oh what the hell," I said, causing them to laugh.

"Here's to you, Riley, and the bright future you have ahead of you." We all clinked our classes together, and the minute my water glass hit the table, I was digging in to the delicious food.

The morning came quick, but that was okay. I was ready to begin the next chapter of my life. I quickly got dressed and dragged Matt out of bed.

"We're going to be running late if you don't get your ass in gear," I said as he groaned at me in annoyance. Once Matt was dressed and ready to go, we made our way downstairs to have breakfast with Angela. I could tell she was upset, but I knew she was happy for me. Once we finished cleaning up from breakfast, Matt and I packed up the last of the things we couldn't pack because we needed them, and we put them in the car.

"Well, this is it," Angela said as we all walked outside.

"This is it," I said back. I could see the tears forming in her eyes, and I knew I wouldn't be too far behind her. She wrapped me in a tight hug as she cried on my shoulder.

"I'm going to miss you so much. You better call me every-day," she said, causing me to laugh.

"I will, I promise."

"And you better call me as soon as you get there," I nodded as Matt gave Angela a hug.

"See you later, Angela. We'll be in touch soon," Matt said as he made his way over to me.

"I love you guys, and have a safe trip," she yelled as we got into the car. We gave her a quick wave.

"Here we go," Matt said, looking at me.

"Here we go," I repeated. He gave me a quick kiss before starting the car and heading down the road. "Here's to the next chapter in our lives," I said as I rolled the window down.